THE CRYPTO-CAPERS
IN
THE CHEST OF MYSTERY

THE CRYPTO–CAPERS
IN
THE CHEST OF
MYSTERY

BOOK 4

Renée Hand

NORTH STAR PRESS OF ST. CLOUD, INC.
St. Cloud, Minnesota

Cover Art and title page by Alla Dubrovich
Text Illustrations by Corinne A. Dwyer

Copyright © 2010 Renée Hand

First Edition: July 2010

ISBN-10: 0-87839-394-3
ISBN-13: 978-0-87839-394-7

Printed in the United States of America.

Published by
North Star Press of St. Cloud, Inc.
P.O. Box 451
St. Cloud, Minnesota 56302
northstarpress.com

Dedication

There are many people I would like to thank. As always, my family is very supportive. I couldn't do what I love to do without them. I want to also thank Jacob Mossing for helping me with the direction of this book. The hours we spent developing ideas were worthwhile ones. I also have new friends of the Crypto-Capers that need to be thanked and recognized. Ben Piazza, Maitland Bowen, and Theryn Bass, all contributed characters for this book. Their characters were of their own creation and I thank them so much for allowing me to use them.

Liliana Stiletti

A Note to the Readers

Welcome to another adventure of the Crypto-Caper Series. I know that after reading *The Legend of the Golden Monkey* you have been eagerly awaiting *The Chest of Mystery*. I believe you are going to enjoy the conclusion of the case. In Book Three you learned about many things, but the one thing that was hanging out, was the knowledge about Mayan numbers. I assure you that, just like the other books in the series, there is always a reason why you are learning new information. Mayan numbers will come in to play in this book, I warned you of that in the beginning of Book Three, so it was very important that you learned about them.

I have mentioned to you before that you will need to keep all the books in the series. I hope you have done that because you will need to refer back to Book Three for information as well as one of the other books in the series in order to use its cipher key to solve the cryptograms in Book Four. Keep following along with the characters in the story because they will guide you through it. As always, pay attention to the hints and clues they give you. You never know what might be important.

As you should have figured out by the picture at the end of Book Three, the Crypto-Capers are going to Pisa, Italy. There are so many amazing things to see there. I will be having various activities on my website to help you learn all you can about some of the sites the Crypto-

Caper team visits. Please check out www.reneeahand.com for that and other information.

Thank you for your continued devotion to this series, and I hope you are enjoying it as much as I am enjoying writing it for you.

Thank you, my friend, for your support—*Grazie, i miei amici, per il vostro supporto.*

The game is afoot, and the Crypto-Capers love a good mystery. Good luck!

Renée Hand

ONE

WITH EYES CLOSED, HIS EARS STILL ringing from the explosion, Maxwell Holmes felt the shift as the plane began its plummet to earth. His stomach rose into his throat, and he felt as if they were on the downhill side of a roller coaster ride—a ride they could not control—or an elevator in freefall. Feeling helpless, though, was not Max's forte. Even with fear trying to grip his chest, he knew he had to keep his senses and be strong. This was no time to panic.

Max opened his eyes, his first rational thought on Mia. Her hands were clenched to the arms of her seat, her face tight with concern as her fingernails dug ever deeper into the armrest cushion, creating full sets of half-moon impressions. Emmanuel was in a similar state of shock and fear. Bent over, his head down, he also had a death-grip on his armrests. Max's eyes slid to Granny, and he paused. She looked barely concerned. Her hands lay relaxed upon the armrests. He smiled in the knowledge that she had already made the choice of remaining calm and not allowing fear to consume her. Instead of waiting for her fate, docile as a lamb or even bawling like a calf on its way to the slaughter, she was taking action. She shouted to Pablo in the cockpit, "How are we looking up there?"

"Not good, Nellie. Both engines are out. We're losing . . . we're losing altitude . . . really fast. We still have cabin pressure. I'm trying to get the engines going . . . but . . . they . . . won't . . . work," boomed Pablo.

"Can you land the plane? I'm more concerned with our landing situation right now than the engines."

Max had to appreciate his grandmother's subtlety. Their landing situation. They were basically falling out of the sky, and his grandmother wanted to know how they could land in the dark.

"Land? The real problem is trying to figure out if I *should* ditch in the ocean or try for land. There's an island ahead. If I can only gain back a glide slope . . . yeah but any kind of landing in the dark . . . I don't like our chances." Pablo shook his head in uncertainty.

Granny pursed her lips, her eyes on the floor of the plane. Max knew she was not one to give up. He found himself hoping she had an ace up her sleeve yet.

"What can we do?" he asked softly. "We don't know where we are, other than over the ocean."

Granny's gaze shifted to his, but she didn't answer his question. Unbelievably, she began to smile. It was as if she remembered something very important.

"We'll be all right, Max. While I still have a fire inside of me, we won't go down this easily." Then Granny began to laugh. "I'm too old to die!"

Max's forehead furrowed and his mouth opened slightly. Granny was the super glue of the group. She was the only one who could hold everyone together without fail. But this sounded a little crazy.

"Um . . . what do you have in mind?" asked Max, hoping she actually had something in mind. The one thing he knew about Granny was that she was a fighter, and if she was going to fight, then so was he.

"Morris?" she said to the fourth member of their team.

Morris, at their home base, was listening, though Max thought he was probably as paralyzed by fear as his sister and Emmanuel. Morris had promised to save them. Max hoped it was within his power to do so.

A shaky voice answered through Granny's watch phone. "Something . . . something disrupted the engines. I don't know exactly what. It's as black as pitch . . . I can't see anything from the satellite . . . nothing . . . just the smoke billowing from the back of the plane." Morris paused briefly, "What happened, Max?"

"I found a tracking device. Figuring it had to be the Panther wanting to keep tabs on us, I put it in water."

"Yes, yes, that should have shorted it out."

"But it didn't. An explosion went off at the back of the plane, triggered, I now believe, by the very short I hoped the water would cause in the tracking device. The engines must've been damaged then." Max's voice trailed off, and he felt another wave of uncertainty grip his insides. The plane was still falling.

"Ahhhh, so someone sabotaged the engines. That'd explain your engine failure and decreasing altitude." Morris's voice trailed off, and Max was sure he could hear him swallowing hard. Then, slowly, Morris continued. "Max, you had no way of knowing. You followed protocol concerning the tracking device. The Panther would have known you'd know how to deactivate it. He must've tweaked it . . . sure, that makes sense. The bomb must've been hidden somewhere near the engines . . . odd that it didn't take out anything else. No, not odd. Your plane going down would look like a simple engine failure or some malfunction, not a planned explosion."

Max sighed and nodded. "If the Panther can't track us, then he wanted to finish us. No, not that. The man was sending us a message."

"A rather pointed one, then."

Max turned and looked at his sister, who was concentrating hard, no longer totally in the grips of her fears. "He's showing us that he's one step ahead."

"It doesn't matter," said Morris. "We have the upper hand. The Panther's still in the Riviera Maya. I'm tracking him. By now he thinks you're dead. He knows his bomb went off. So, now it's up to us to finish what we have started." Morris's tone was not entirely optimistic.

"How?" piped in Mia, her voice filled with frustration and lack of hope. "How can we finish what we have started when we're still in a plane spiraling down in a vortex of wind and speed to the ocean? We're going to die and probably quickly. I don't want it to end this way."

Morris's tone became serious. "End? How well do you know me, Mia?"

The question was an easy one, and yet Mia couldn't answer it. She was filled with fear and uncertainty, but the biggest crippler was doubt. For once in her life, she doubted they could be saved.

"I love you guys," said Morris. "You're family to me. More than anything, you need to know that if there's something I can do to help you prepare for every situation, I'd do it, will do it . . . have *done* it—even if it wasn't with *all* of you knowing."

"I think . . ." Mia started, her biting tone evident, but then after several seconds, her features relaxed. Her mind started to become clear, and confidence once again filled her chest. Her expression lightened, and tears sprang to her eyes. "Oh, Morris, you have a way!"

"You know I do. In your heart, I need you to believe it. Gather your wits about you and believe that I'll save you, Mia. Can you do that for me?"

Max knew what Morris was doing, and he saw Mia's resolve strengthen. Mia had looked like she was losing her mind. If she did that, just the experience, assuming they lived, could've scarred her for life. Max appreciated his friend for what he was doing.

Morris's voice now switched back to Granny's watch phone. "I'm always prepared for the worse. My fear of flying stems from the fact that planes are precarious and uncontrollable. That being said, I authorized a few 'adjustments' to Pablo's plane when it was at the hanger at that private airport waiting for you guys in Las Vegas. Remember, Granny?" All eyes were on Granny now. Max remembered that she had forced them into seeing the sights and shopping for two agonizing days when he just wanted to be off on the next leg of the adventure. She had known, then, known what Morris was up to but had distracted them with looking for souvenirs during the time the plane was being worked on.

"I had a friend of ours help us out and make the adjustments to the plane we needed before you left."

"A friend of ours?" commented Max sarcastically. "You mean, a friend of Maggie Devereaux."

"My cousin helped us?" spouted Spencer from the front of the plane, suddenly coming out of his stupor and joining the conversation.

"This is great, and all, Morris," shouted Pablo from the cockpit, "but we're still *falling!*"

"Ah, yes, I digress," said Morris. "Pablo, there's a large red button on your right. Now would be a good time to press it!"

Max, who could see into the cockpit, watched as Pablo searched for the button. Then his eyes fixed on a now-pulsing, circular red button.

Pablo reached toward the button and glanced quickly over at Spencer. "Just in case this doesn't work, you know I love you, right?"

"I love you, too, Pablo!" Spencer squeaked and gave his brother a weak smile before Max saw Pablo press the button.

Max didn't know exactly what to expect. He heard something overhead, like a cargo door open. Then there was a *whoosh*, and his seatbelt suddenly gripped him, as the downward plunge slowed. The plane, its nose pointed down after the explosion, leveled out, and he knew with certainty that they'd be okay. He didn't, however, hear the roar of engines, so there weren't backups.

"What happened?" Morris shouted. "Did it work? Did it work? You guys okay? Talk to me."

"Well," said Max, "something sure did . . . but what? We still don't have power."

"Team," Morris said with proud satisfaction, "you now are riding under a parachute attached to the plane. It's a rather large, amazingly strong, parachute. Actually, it's a bit more than that. It's more like a hot-air balloon. Pablo, pump the red button to control jets of flame into it to keep you aloft. That should help you control your landing without too much damage to the plane or to you. There's an island in front of you. I recommend aiming for it. You'll be landing somewhere near the Azores, off Portugal. It's a group of islands so choose the one nearest. The exact island you'll be landing on, I believe, might be St. Miguel.

"Now, Pablo, its a rather small island. If you miss it, well . . . you could be landing in the ocean instead. The balloon really wasn't meant to carry a plane. It's not a zeplon or anything. So your altitude is still slipping. Otherwise, I'd say take it all the way to Italy. Sorry about that!"

Max, Granny and Mia glanced at each other and shook their heads.

Morris said, "I'm dispatching a friend who just happens to be on holiday on St. Miguel. He's familiar with the area, so he'll be able to help you. He'll find you and help get repairs to the plane organized, so you guys can continue. Just wait for him.

"Pablo, I'll help guide you in by satellite. In this darkness, you won't be able to see a thing. But in a few hours it'll be dawn. Try not to wander off too far. You'll be in unfamiliar territory until I can see what's around you. And, team, make sure that Emmanuel, Spencer, and Pablo are with at least one of you at all times, if you need to leave the plane. I can track the three of you easily, but them, not so much."

"Understood!" replied Max, thinking about that problem as well.

"How are we to know who this friend is?" asked Mia, finally calmed down enough to be inquisitive.

Morris laughed. "Oh, don't worry. You'll know. Contact me after you've landed, and Granny . . ."

"Yes, Morris dear?"

"You might want to brush up on your Portuguese. You might need it."

Morris's voice dissolved, and the passengers stared at each other in amazement, still in awe at what had transpired in the last few minutes. They weren't going to die in a plummeting airplane. They went from almost crashing to a new lease on life. Though Spencer and Emmanuel were still looking pretty terrified, the Crypto-Capers were not the usual passengers on an airplane, flying or falling. They were used to such the tricks of fate and were very adaptable to any situation. It always seemed that they knew just what to do to survive, even at times when their strength faltered. The one thing they could count on in any situation—was each other. And on that dark night over the Atlantic Ocean that surely included Morris.

TWO

PABLO, WATCHING HIS INSTRUMENTS, depressed the red button rather frequently. Each time, the passengers heard a *whoosh* as the flames shot out from the top of the plane and kept the parachute/balloon holding them up from sinking too quickly. An hour later the passengers glanced out their windows, staring into the thin light of early pre-dawn as they waited for the landing they knew was coming. They watched the ocean loom closer and closer. Pablo tried to steer them to safety. Though the landing was more or less out of his control and up to the winds pushing them, he was able to direct their course in some small sense with his flaps and the tail of the plane. They saw the island and leaned toward it, hoping to help the plane with their effort. Pablo hoped they could reach the clearing they approached.

As the plane settled lower and lower despite the flames, the ocean developed waves, and the swells often broke out into whitecaps. They sure didn't want to go down in the water.

Max glanced hastily at Granny, who was still surprisingly calm, certainly not as tense as the rest of them.

As his focus flitted to his sister, she seemed to relax suddenly. Max looked out the window and whispered a little prayer as the wind gusted and blew them in-land, past the crashing waves on the beach. Over land, Pablo leaned pretty heavily on the gas, inflating the balloon often, and they lifted over a line of rugged mountains before settling into a valley where it seemed they would be landing.

"That's the last of the fuel," said Pablo. "Now we have to go down. Might be a hard landing. Brace yourselves!"

As the airplane descended, Max watched the ground rush up to meet them. It was a hard landing. Even though Granny told them to assume the crash position, even though the wheels collapsed upon impact, the belly of the plane smacked the ground hard enough to burst seams all along the sides of the plane. A number of windows shattered. The sound of metal grinding and buckling roared in their ears. Then it got very still.

Max popped open one eyelid, raised his head and peered around. All the lights had gone out, and it was pitch black in the plane. But he could hear Granny taking a few deep breaths, and Emmanuel whimpering from his seat.

"Everyone okay?" Max asked. His voice was thin and shaky. He cleared his throat and asked the question again. "Morris, you dear sweet paranoid geek, we're down and alive."

"Good to know," said Morris, sounding very relieved.

Then Pablo shouted from the cockpit, "We have officially landed, folks. It's now safe to move about the cabin." Then he laughed.

Mia let out a strangled giggle.

Max unlocked his seatbelt and heard the others follow suit. He retrieved his backpack and without delay fished out his flashlight and checked the rest of the contents. Other lights snapped on, and he knew that Granny and Mia were doing the same.

"Well, I have a broken magnifying glass, but that's it. What about you, Mia?"

Mia was still digging in her bag, moving things around. "I'm good here. Nothing broken. You, Granny?"

Granny surveyed her bag thoroughly. "The glass from my picture frame of me and Reggie is smashed to bits, but otherwise, nothing else is damaged."

"That's good to hear!" commented Max as he carefully pulled bits of glass from his bag.

Granny picked broken glass from the inside of her bag as well. Mia squinted out the window into the darkness.

"What should we do?" she asked.

"Well, dawn'll be here soon. I think we should rest, maybe even sleep, until we know what we are dealing with," answered Max.

"I agree with Max," said Pablo. "We've landed, we're safe, and, for the time being, that's enough for me."

Max, Granny, and Mia eased back their seats and closed their eyes. After a few minutes, Pablo, Spencer, and Emmanuel rested as well.

The only one who couldn't really rest was Max. Behind his closed lids, his mind was racing with the latest events. He spent the next couple hours staring out his window, his fingers on his lips, deep in thought. He watched as the sky continued to lighten. Stars winked out. The sky grew grey, then white, then washed with blue. Then he saw it, a bright ray of light glint through the window opposite him. He could feel the heat as it splayed across his arm like paint on a canvas, then moved lazily down to his hand with a tender stroke.

The sun, like an alarm clock, woke everyone on the plane. Pablo and Spencer stood up and began to explore the damage to the inside of the cabin. Emmanuel was up as well, trying to force open the bathroom door. Mia and Granny stood just as Max did and stretched. He shrugged. "Well, no point in us just standing here. Let's see where we landed." Granny grabbed Emmanuel, telling him he could pee outside, and guided him along to the door just behind the cockpit. He stumbled with his first few steps, still a little shook up, but was soon coming around as his feet moved forward. Pablo and Spencer opened the door. Using the flattened landing gear as a ladder, they climbed down into the wild grasses.

"Let's see the damage," said Pablo as he headed for the wing of the plane. The group followed briskly behind, curious about what they were going to find as well. Max glanced at their environment. It appeared that they had landed near a thickly forested area. Grass, greener than Ireland's rolling hills, filled the rest of the valley.

Giant azaleas, cannas, and hydrangeas grew from hedgerows and along the margins of the woods.

Max looked around further. They were in a large bowl. Surrounding them were tall mountains with trees scattered down their sides. The floor of the valley was made up of fields and meadows. He recognized box-wood trees, ginkgo and monkey trees, palm and pine trees. Max almost felt as if he were on a science fiction world and not an island off the Portugal coast.

The temperature was mild in comparison to the Riviera Maya. There was no humidity.

In silence, the group walked toward the back of the plane and looked up. They could see clearly the absent, partially destroyed, engine and the black residue surrounding the entire area. Max ran his fingers through his hair as he focused his gaze on what remained of the left engine.

"It definitely looks like a bomb went off here," Max said, knowing Morris listened. "Not a large one because it didn't affect anything else around it, didn't breach the interior, but it certainly was big enough to destroy the engine."

Pablo then moved hastily around the tail of the plane to the right engine. It looked to be in the same condition as the left—partially destroyed and shaped into a crescent moon. "The person who placed the bombs here knew what they were doing. The intent was to take us down." Pablo's face was tight with concern, probably knowing his plane might not be salvaged.

"Who had access to the plane?" asked Granny.

"Anyone at the airfield," responded Pablo with a shrug. "Those bombs could have been there for days. When—"

Max had held up his right hand, causing Pablo to pause.

"Wait a minute, Pablo. Let's think about this a minute. The Panther flies into the Riviera Maya, hears from one of his accomplices that we're flying to Machu Picchu, which he set up by leaving the Yupana for us to find. He puts the bombs in the engine as a backup in case we get in the way and things don't work out as he planned. He had someone plant the tracking device where I'd find it. So far, I believe our assumptions are correct. Looking at the damage, I do believe this is what happened. It explains so much."

"That's definitely plausible," said Mia, "but how did the Panther know what plane we were going to use? He had no way of knowing that."

Max waggled a finger at her. "He would if he used Walter as a go-between. Yes, that makes perfect sense. Walter had to have told the Panther which plane to put the bomb on."

"Otherwise the plane Walter was piloting would have been sabotaged as well." The remark came from Spencer. It was the first time he had spoken since landing. All eyes turned to him. Max opened his mouth to voice a question, but before he could say anything, Morris chimed in.

"I know what you are thinking, team, but let me fill you in. The plane Walter was piloting didn't go down. He and the fat man were arrested in Peru when they landed. It was only then they realized that they'd been duped by us. The Panther is still at large, but all of his accomplices, and you already know of Marissa Sanchez's arrest, were taken into custody."

That cleared up most of Max's concerns.

By the time they were finished analyzing the damage to the plane, Emmanuel, who had been watching intently what everyone was doing, noticed someone coming towards them on a little grey donkey.

"Max?" he said tentatively. "Someone's coming."

Max, Granny, and Mia instantly gazed in the direction Emmanuel was looking. The trio stepped forward, half blocking and, therefore, protecting, Pablo, Spencer, and Emmanuel.

"Who do you think that is?" asked Mia, moving closer to her brother's side. "A local?"

"He might be the one sent to help us. Morris?"

"Can't tell. My contact is a tourist, so he'd have to have hired the donkey."

"I can't imagine that he'd just happen to be in the middle of nowhere in case someone needed help." Max remarked sarcastically, as he glanced back at Mia and then at Granny, awaiting her to take the next step.

Granny waited until the man was close enough to hear her before she stepped forward. "*Dia bom a você, senhor. Você por um acaso fala inglês?*"

The man looked at Granny in curiosity as she asked him in Portuguese if he spoke English. "Sim, faço, ma'am. Your accent is remarkable. How can I help you?"

"As you can see, we've been in an crash and need help." Granny partially turned towards the plane. "Our plane went down and—"

"Is anyone hurt?" the man asked quickly as his ocean-blue eyes scanned the plane behind them, his attention concentrating on the parachute/balloon that had collapsed and lay on the ground like a huge tarp next to the plane.

"No, thank goodness. No one was hurt. We are, however, in need of some guidance."

Granny waited. Max knew she hoped this was their contact and that he would say so. Though he believed they had, momentarily at least, outwitted the Panther, there was a chance the crafty criminal was still ahead of them. This man could be their contact, or he could be an assassin sent by the Panther to finish the job.

The man eased his donkey past Granny. "You know, I like that parachute. It was a very clever idea." The man dismounted his donkey and stood in front of them. He was a good-looking man with burnt-orange hair, brown-rimmed glasses, and freckles splashed across his nose and face. His features were kind and calm. His built was slender, yet strong.

"Yes, it was," inserted Mia, without elaborating on exactly what the parachute was and how it had not only saved their lives but gotten them to land. "The one who came up with it should be given a gold medal and a pat on the back for an outstanding job." Mia eyed the man suspiciously, waiting to see how he would respond.

He smiled. "Those are kind words, but in all fairness, it's easy to spot the author of this clever work. My name is Benjamin Piazza. My friends call me, Ben. I was sent here by Morris to help you."

THREE

"I'M MIA. THIS IS MY BROTHER, Max, and our grand-mother, Nellie Holmes. These are our friends, Pablo, Spencer, and Emmanuel."

Ben smiled and nodded to each person as Mia pointed each out. "What a pleasure it is to meet you all," he said pleasantly. "Now, what do you need me to do?"

Max gave a little laugh and looked at the donkey. "What *can* you do? Morris didn't tell us about your skills."

"Oh, guys," came Morris's disembodied voice, "Ben's very knowledgeable about cars, planes, trains . . . you name it. His talents at manipulating parts to suit his needs is what impresses me the most."

Ben gave a little bow. "Thank you, Morris."

Granny lifted her wrist. "Just out of curiosity, Morris dear, how did you meet Ben?" she asked.

"His father is a friend of my father's—you know the drill. It is a small world. That about says it."

Many times that saying has proven true, and no one knew it better than the Crypto-Capers.

"Good enough," said Pablo. He rested a hand on the fusilage of his plane. "Is there any way you can fix this? This is *my* plane. If there is any way you can salvage it, I'd greatly appreciate it."

Ben climbed up on the left wing to inspect the damage. "By the look of the engines alone . . . well, there is no way I would be able to fix this, but they can be replaced. I don't have the parts, though, and getting them will take weeks. Perhaps longer."

The group glanced at each other and then all eyes focused on Max. Pablo sighed. "We really don't have weeks to spare. Too much can happen . . . we'd lose all we've gained."

Ben nodded his head in understanding, though Max doubted Morris would have told him much more than what he needed to know.

"And, I'm thinking, you don't want to destroy the plane further, yeah? Is your plane not insured? Because, to be quite honest, there's no way you'll be getting it out of here any time soon."

Ben then glanced at the rest of the group. "You do know where you are, don't you? These are the Azores, several islands to the west of Portugal. This is Sao Miguel, and though this island is beautiful and full of mystery, it's still an island in the middle of nowhere. Look around. This isn't a safe haven. Those mountains sometimes billow with volcanic smoke and tremors occur frequently. We're near the center of a volcanic crater, the Sete Cidades Crater. This area is full of volcanic activity, bubbling lagoons, and hot springs. To the east is where we need to go, to the small village of Sete Cidades. The half-moon lagoon you came over is part of the crater. But as beautiful as this countryside is, as tantalizing as the lagoons may seem, this is still a dangerous, if awe-inspiring, place. To make matters more interesting for us, these islands sit at the meeting place of cyclones and violent storms, and the weather report says that one is on its way."

Pablo looked sadly at his damaged aircraft.

"I heard a warning last night. We have maybe a day to get you out of here. The airfields" and he waved his hand in the general direction of the village, "will be preparing for the storm already. They'll only allow so many planes out today. Then they'll ground all air traffic, letting no one in or out of Sao Miguel. And, unfortunately, there's no way we'll be able to get to the airfield before the airport shuts down."

At first, the group just looked at each other, realizing that they left one life-threatening situation for another. Then all eyes focused on Pablo. After several minutes of assessing the situation, he looked at Ben, who was waiting patiently for a response, a plan of action, something.

"You made your point, Ben. Crystal clear. Do what you need to do to get us out of here safely."

Ben smacked his hands together, and a wide, satisfied grin spread across his face, clumping the freckles on his cheeks. Straight white teeth gleamed at them.

"That's the spirit!" he chortled. Ben moved quickly to his donkey and patted its back. "We'll need to hike through this valley and up those big hills there."

Everyone's head turned as Ben pointed towards the hill. It looked rocky and the path twisty and steep.

"On the other side is the tourist town of Sete Cidades, which I was telling you about. I have a van there. Morris contacted me several hours ago. It's taken me this long to reach you, but the route from this side is a steeper climb. We need to be on our way, and we need to move quickly. I brought the donkey in case—"

Max smiled. Ben had turned to Granny, but she had given him the most withering look back.

"—in case someone was injured," Ben finished tactfully. "Twisted ankles can slow us down."

Granny gave him a small smile and nod.

Ben jumped down from the plane's wing and took a couple steps in the direction of the donkey. When no one began to move, he turned back. "Shall we go?"

His words jolted the group to life. Granny quickly took charge. "Right. Okay, everyone. Make sure you have everything we need."

Everyone began checking gear.

"We can save the donkey and walk, Ben," Granny said, "though it's gracious of you to be so thoughtful. However, could the donkey carry our bags?"

"Oh, sure. Donkeys are very strong," said Ben.

Granny said to Max, "Is there anything we're forgetting inside of the plane, dear?"

Max nodded. He hastily grabbed Emmanuel by the arm, and they raced quickly back inside of the plane for their equipment bag and luggage.

When Max returned with several bags, Ben smiled and motioned to him as he pulled some rope from a leather pouch. He quickly tied the handles of the bags with a length of rope between them so he could sling them across the donkey's back. When he had them in place, he ran another length of rope from the handles around the donkey's chest to the other side and secured it to the handles of the bags on that side. He ran another line around the animal's rear under its tail and secured that again on the other side. In this way the ups and down of a mountain trail, would not dislodge the load on the donkey's back and prevent a constant shifting from chafing the animal's skin. And though the little donkey looked rather overburdened, Ben assured them that it could handle the load with ease.

Fortunately for the donkey, the only luggage on the plane was what had belonged to the Crypto-Capers. The rest of the group hadn't had a chance to pack much. Pablo and Spencer had only stashed a few essentials into a backpack from their earlier false trip to Machu Picchu.

Ben glanced at the group. "Are we set then?"

Pablo, Emmanuel, and Spencer nodded. Granny, Mia and Max, who had retained their personal backpacks, adjusted the straps over their shoulders and nodded. Spencer had his small backpack in place.

But Ben didn't move. He was staring at the large parachute fluttering on the ground. "I brought some water for us to drink," he said, vaguely indicating the leather pouch also tied to the donkey, "so if anyone needs some, just holler."

Then he turned to Pablo and Granny in turn, his look suddenly intense. "I was just thinking. With a big storm coming in, I fear the parachute could be a problem. If it was strong enough to get you safely here, it might fill with wind and lift the plane again. I think we need to secure it inside the plane." Ben recruited the group to help him fold the parachute into a long loose bundle, like a rolled-up rug. With everyone's help, they muscled the parachute inside the plane and carefully closed the doors.

As Pablo completed this, Max spoke to Morris through his watch phone to let them know what was going on.

"Daylight is a gift. I've been watching you by satellite since dawn broke. Be careful on your hike. Don't let Granny hurt herself. There are crevices and fistulas in most of the rock formations. Wouldn't want anyone to break a leg, you know. I've been keeping an eye on the storm. Unfortunately it's going to hit sooner than expected. You have until nightfall to get out of there and get to someplace safe. And, Max, these are usually really bad storms. Caught in the open, you'd be in serious trouble. I need to impress upon you the importance of your hurrying."

Granny had leaned close to Max. "The warning is noted," she said. "We'll move as fast as we can."

Ben said, "All set?" Upon hearing no objections, he continued with, "Let's go!"

The warm sun showered them with light. The grasses in the valley were tall, making even this relatively level part of the journey challenging. Ben led the way with the donkey, which seemed to carry its burden with ease. The valley was wide, and then they had to start up the hills. It took them several hours to reach the peak of the first steep rise. When they did, they were all out of breath and exhausted. The climb had been strenuous. But the grasses were shorter here. Flowers bloomed everywhere, and plants of infinite variety grew up around the enormous rocks, looking like paintings framed in stone.

On the top of the ridge, their passage evened out, becoming easier, if only for a time.

Mia caught her breath and began to enjoy the walk. This awakened some curiosity about their guide. "What are you doing on this island, Ben?" she asked him.

He glanced back and smiled. "I'm on vacation."

"Really?"

He nodded. "In my regular job, I take apart and reconstruct various mechanical things. When I go on vacation . . . well, I find it difficult to stop my creativity from flowing."

Mia, as well as Spencer and Emmanuel, who had taken an interest in the conversation, waited for Ben to tell them exactly what kind of work he did.

Ben laughed. "Oh, no, no, no. Don't ask me any particulars. I'm technically sworn to secrecy." With that, Ben smiled brilliantly and continued on the way, chuckling to himself as he did.

When they turned to see how far they had come, they were amazed at the beauty of the landscape. The area was vast and green. Forests softened the mountainsides, and grasses waved like water in the valleys. So many bold and beautiful flowers bloomed that the island looked like a wild garden. But the breeze that rushed at them was beginning to bow the flowers and make the grasses wave. The sky to the west had darkened and filled with inky clouds, though overhead, the sun still shone.

The group then turned and gazed at what was to come—another rocky slope and winding path down to the valley, but this was not acres of wild grasses, but rocks, tall rambling plants, and trees. The terrain as well was quite different and yet beautiful in its own way. They could see the two lagoons far below, as well as the village off to the right. A road wound its way around the lagoons. As Ben led the way down the hill, the others were hopeful that the worst of their journey was done.

FOUR

As THEY BEGAN THEIR DESCENT, Ben pointed out the lagoons. "The scenery is magnificent here. It's one of the reasons I vacation in the Azores. Those two lagoons are called Lagoa Verde, which means, literally, Green Lake, and Lagoa Azul, Blue Lake."

"Why are they different colors?" asked Granny.

"That's a very good question. Scientifically speaking, I think it has something to do with the minerals leached into the water from the magma far below. But, I choose the more romantic explanation. These are magic waters. The legend attributes the different colors of the waters to tears shed by a princess and a shepherd who wept when their love was thwarted and they were transformed into the two lakes at the bottom of the crater."

"That's sweet," whispered Mia.

Ben glanced back and smiled. "I thought you ladies would like that."

Nothing else was said for the next few hours as they put all of their energy into their hike. Though they were headed downward, the path was far from easy. They often had to cross rock fields and make their way down steep slopes where a misstep could send them tumbling. As it was, Emmanuel ripped his pants at the knees and had a bad scrape on his right knee, and Spencer's shirt had torn when it caught on a shrub. Though Granny had kept up rather impressively, she was beginning to look a bit pale and tired by the time they reached the road.

With the sound of thunder in the hills behind them, and the sun now at the edge of dark clouds, they didn't pause, but swiftly headed towards the village. At least their path was easier. The closer they got to the village the more charming and picturesque it became. Sete Cidades had curious Spanish-influenced houses and a nineteenth-century neo-gothic church. It also had green pastures and a modest, attractive lake Ben called Santiago. Next to Lagoa Azul, they passed an amazing garden filled with magnificent trees and masses of whimsically trimmed azaleas.

The group was exhausted, sweaty, dirty, as well as hungry. They trudged down the middle of the road until they reached Ben's van, a full-sized Volkswagen. Wordlessly, they helped him unload the donkey and stow everything into the back of the van. When that was accomplished, Ben led the donkey towards a barn at the edge of a pasture. He hailed an older man working there and handed him the donkey's lead. Max and Mia could hear him speaking to the man in Portuguese.

"What's he saying, Granny?" whispered Max.

"He's thanking the man for allowing him to use the donkey for the day," replied Granny. "He also hoped that the man's wife was feeling better."

Max glanced at the man closer, studying him. Older, definitely in his seventies, his rough appearance spoke of his dedication to his animals. The way he rubbed the donkey's forehead and gave it water showed his love for the animal. To Max it seemed as if the beast was more a family member than just a pack animal. Mia broke into Max's thoughts.

"My feet hurt so badly," she moaned loudly.

"My legs too," added Spencer.

"You can actually feel your legs?" piped in Emmanuel. "My knees hurt, though."

"We're all tired," supplied Max tersely as he rubbed his lower back. While they waited for Ben to return, Max updated Morris, letting him know that they'd reached the village safely and were doing okay.

"I see. Thanks for the update. Make sure someone ices Emmanuel's knees before you all collapse. Oh, Max, I'm going to be out of contact for a little while. My dad was called back to Italy for a job, and I'm going to help him. I'll still be able to hear you through my IPOD . . . I . . . er . . . modified it a tad. I'm bringing my laptop, so I'll still be able to control everything wherever I am. I'll meet up with you and the rest of the team in Pisa. You're in good hands with Ben. He'll make sure you get to where you need to go. Trust him!"

Everyone else had moved to the fence along the road, watching Ben and the old man chat. Max crossed to the other side of the road, making sure he was out of their earshot.

"We do trust him, Morris. He's proven his worth. But, dear friend, don't do anything foolish in Italy, I beg you. You know what I'm talking about."

Max paused for a moment, allowing his words to sink in. "You know what happened the last time you decided to become adventurous and join us in the field. You could have gotten caught putting that GPS chip into the back of the Panther's neck. You have no idea how dangerous that man is. You took a huge risk. I commend you for your bravery, but please, don't do anything rash like that again, unless you have us there to support you. It is easy for you to get hurt going solo."

"I have the element of surprise on my side, Max. No one, not even the Panther, will be expecting me to leave London."

"Morris," Max said.

"Look, I know that I'm not as knowledgeable in the field as the rest of you. I'm thin—I'm not in any way athletic. I have allergies and enough phobias to keep myself at home forever, but I liked that taste of adventure every once in a while. Anyway, my dad needs help."

"Like the taste of adventure," said Max, his tone going from warning to mocking.

"Okay, fine," said Morris. "I really don't like adventure at all. I feel much more secure behind the scenes, and frankly you, Mia, and Granny do the field work because you're so good at it. But—"

"No, Morris, you misunderstand what I'm saying. I don't think you're weak or incapable. None of us do. In fact, you have more strength than all of us put together. You have abilities, I could never have. But, just like you watch over us every day when we're on a case, we watch over you as well. You're a valuable part of this team, and we care for you. We want you to be safe, that's all, and believe it or not, we do appreciate you." Max laughed briefly.

"Max—" Morris's voice broke. It took him several seconds to get control again. "That means a lot to me, mate. It's just that sometimes I think . . ." Morris switched topics, so he wouldn't have to say anything else. "Ah, thanks! I'll be careful."

"But why take the risk?"

"Because we desperately need an edge with the Panther. He's so smart, so clever . . . well mostly he has a lot more resources than we do right now. We have to throw him a curve."

"I know, but—"

"Now, I have been keeping track of the storm. I hoped you'd reach the village sooner, but you should have plenty of time to get to shelter before that storm hits. Don't doddle, though. I'll connect with you again soon, once we're in Pisa, if not before. I'll be listening periodically to check on your progress. Talk to you soon."

"Be safe, Morris, and you're welcome." Max turned around. Mia was watching him and gave him a questioning glance. Max shook his head and smiled. He knew his sister wanted to speak with him, but before she could, Ben returned. Everyone piled into the van. Before he got in, Ben fetched water bottles from a cooler in the back of the van and handed everyone a bottle. Nothing but the slurping and gulping of water followed until a collective loud, "Ah!"

Ben started up the van and pulled out onto the road. "I have a house a short jaunt from here. It's very secluded. We'll rest there before we leave again."

"Where will we be going?" asked Pablo.

"Portugal. Isn't that your destination?"

"Not exactly," said Max smoothly. Ben glanced at Max through his rearview mirror.

As they drove away from Sete Cidades, Ben said, "You don't have to tell me anything specific about your case, or what you're working on precisely, but it would be helpful if you gave me the location of where you needed to go. Then I can serve you better."

Max and Mia waited for Granny to give the particulars. Though she had slumped down in her seat, glad to be finished with the hike, she straightened herself up. "We're headed for Pisa, Italy. We have some business there." Granny smiled politely, looking again calm and cool.

"All of you?" inquired Ben.

"Well, no!" said Pablo. "Spencer needs to get back to the Riviera Maya."

"You're sure?" asked Granny. "You're welcome to come with us."

"No, no," said Spencer. "I'm positive! My parents are coming for me. I'll be safe in the United States with them."

"And I need to take care of my plane," said Pablo. "I just can't leave it there to rot. I'm sure salvaging it will take some time . . . won't it Ben?"

"I fear it will. And there's nothing we can do until after this storm passes, and bad storms can last days. I'll notify island authorities. It'll definitely take more than a day to hash out. After we get the others on their way, you two must stay with me. We'll be safe there during the storm. Then I can take you and Spencer to the airport where you can send him on his way back to Mexico, or you can rent a plane if you need to take him yourself. You'll only able to do that on this island."

"Thanks, Ben. We'll take you up on that." Pablo looked relieved.

"And what of the rest of us?" asked Emmanuel.

"I'll take you to Portugal where you can get a plane for Pisa," replied Ben.

"And how are we going to get there? I thought you said that there were no planes going out with the storm."

"Oh, that's true, Emmanuel. But, I said nothing about us leaving on a plane, did I?" Ben chuckled.

Emmanuel looked confused. Ben looked back and winked at him. "You'll have to wait and see what I have up my sleeve."

FIVE

BEFORE LONG, BEN PULLED off the road down a narrow dirt road barely more than two tire tracks to the left. It didn't look like much. The entrance was almost hidden behind wild grasses and thick shrubs and tipped sharply downward. Granny held fast to the seat in anticipation as they pitched down a hill through a wall of trees. Once beyond the screen of trees, Granny and others sucked in their breaths at the beauty hidden from the road. Ben had a beautiful stone house, built partially into the hillside, and nestled among plantings of exquisite flowers and backed by massive basalt formations. The driveway swung around to the front of the small but lovely place. But as quaint as the house looked, solar panels on the roof hinted at a more modern interior.

Ben parked, and everyone eased out of the van, wanting to see more, but still feeling the effects of their hike. The group followed Ben up wooden steps to a covered porch. As he approached the front door, Max noticed that he didn't remove a key, but instead leaned forward towards a red panel and let it scan his eye. Max was impressed.

"Are you and Morris related? Because I swear you're just as brilliant as he is," Max said.

Ben turned and smiled as they heard the door unlock. Everyone followed Ben when he walked inside.

"Saves me from having—and/or losing—a key," he said, "and this is a lot more secure. The windows and doors are made of reinforced steel and glass, so the chances someone could break in are minuscule. Plus the security system for the house is quite complex. Good luck to anyone foolish enough to try."

Ben led them to the kitchen, which was enormous. It had an open design with a marble countertop on the center island. Stools around it offered seating. "Feel free to make yourself at home," Ben told them. "Lights!" he called to no one in particular. Lights came on. "This house is very energy efficient. The power comes from the sun . . . you probably noticed the solar panels on the roof. Everything is automated. The water only turns on if it senses something underneath a faucet. So no water waste. Toilets work the same way. I even have air blowers installed instead of hand towels or paper towels, so again, minimum waste."

"I'm moving in," declared Granny.

"Me, too," joined in Mia.

Ben laughed as he filled glasses with cool water. He arranged crackers and cheese on a plate and added some fruit sitting in a bowl on the counter. By the time he was finished, the light meal he had provided was enough to make their hungry mouths water.

"Here you go!" Ben said, pushing the plates towards them across the counter. "Please, dive in. It's not much, but I hope it'll tide you over until we reach Portugal. It's almost six o'clock. I figure we have just enough time for this snack, a bit of freshening up, then we should be going. The trip should take little over an hour."

All hands rushed to the plates of food, with no regard for the nicities of plates and napkins. They ate like ravenous wolves, devouring every morsel. By the time they were done, not a crumb remained.

After that, everyone took a turn in the bathroom and cleaned up. Once everyone was refreshed and ready, they headed outside. Pablo and Spencer had retrieved their backpacks and placed them in one of Ben's spare bedrooms while the others took turns using the bathroom. Finished, they went outside where Emmanuel and Max were waiting.

"Are you and Pablo going to be all right here?" asked Emmanuel as he closed the door to the van and returned to the porch.

"Are you kidding? This is a really neat house. I don't mind staying here," answered Spencer.

"I know," continued Emmanuel, "but . . ."

Max leaned toward him. "I think he's trying to see if you'd like to come with us. You've helped us out so much, Spencer. We hate to leave you here."

Spencer smiled his shy smile, feeling very honored to have been a part of the group, even for a short while.

"Once we get everything situated with the plane, we'll be heading back to the Riviera Maya," said Pablo. "My parents should be there to take him to Las Vegas."

"I'm glad that I could help Mia—you—I mean, the *team*," stammered Spencer. "I'm glad I could help *the team* with this case."

Max glanced at Emmanuel, and they both shared a silent chuckle.

"You know," Max whispered, "if you asked my sister for her e-mail address, I'm sure she'd give it to you. The case isn't over yet. We still might need your help."

Spencer shook his head, then nodded, then did a combination of the two. Max laughed. Ben came out with Granny's luggage and the equipment bag. As they waited for Granny and Mia to join them on the porch, Spencer said, "Do you think she'd give it to me?"

Before Max could reply, Mia, Granny, and Ben came out the front door. They made a pile of the luggage. When each of them had shouldered their packs and bags they all—including Pablo and Spencer—followed Ben, not to the van as Max supposed, but up a trail on the other side of the driveway. The trail led away from the house and dropped down to the ocean. Compared to the workout hike they had already taken that day, this was an easy stroll. The only concern was the growl of thunder that sounded closer than before. As they reached a soft sandy beach, they noticed a cave. Ben walked directly toward it.

The cave was a black hole—a silent, toothy mouth open in the face of the rocky cliff. The group

paused, almost not wanting to follow Ben, but Granny
pushed them forward, quietly chastising them for their
fears. Ben fearlessly led the way through the mouth into
the dark depths of the cave. Hanging from the roof, like
enormous diamonds, were huge, shimmering stalactites.
As they focused their attention on the bottom of the
cave, where a river flowed out into the ocean.

Ben led them along a path that followed the river
back into the hill. The cave was a winding, underground
maze of low, dark tunnels. At times they had to duck
down where the ceiling leaned down nearly to the surface
of the water. Then they left the river and turned down
another tunnel that led them steadily downward again
and opened up to a bay, though still inside the mouth of
a wider cave. The sand beneath their feet was pearly white
and soft. They made their way around a promontory of
stone to a dock where a hovercraft was docked.

"You have a hovercraft?" exclaimed Mia. "Is this what we're taking to Portugal?"

"Yup," said Ben. "Built it myself. It took me around three hundred hours, too. Definitely more than just one stretch of vacation time, I'll tell you that."

"It's a platform hovercraft, isn't it?" said Max.

Ben grinned. "Indeed, and it can carry up to eighteen-hundred pounds, or ten or more passengers. I often haul cargo back and forth from Portugal and some of the nearby islands."

He then turned to Spencer and Pablo. "Now, Pablo, I already showed you some of the inside features of my house. After we leave, go back there and relax. It's sheltered by the cliff, and I've never had any storm damage there except to the landscaping. It'll be dark in a few hours. If Morris is right, the storm will hit soon. Lock up like I showed you and keep an eye out. If you have any trouble—I'm thinking more by way of intruders than the storm—I want you to come down here into the caves. Lots safer. There's a passage through the basement. By the wall over there I have a box of flashlights, batteries, candles, food, water, and blankets. There's enough there to keep you both safe for days. I've camped down here many times when we get really bad storms or I just need to disappear for a while. The water might raise a bit but don't worry about that. If you feel threatened in any way, over by that wall is a key—turn it. It'll close a stone panel and protect you. Any questions?"

Pablo and Spencer shook their heads.

"Good! If I'm not back in a few hours, then I have gotten detained. If the storm hits before I come back, I'll hole up someplace on the mainland. Now I'll let you say your good-byes." Ben then strode down to the hovercraft to get it ready.

Granny had already told Pablo how much he had meant to their team when they were in the house, so she only embraced Pablo again, then hugged Spencer, patting him on the head. There were no tears in her eyes, though Max knew she felt the emotion of their parting. *Anyway,* he told himself, *she's already expressed the notion that we'll probably be seeing them again.*

Emmanuel had said his good-byes and walked to the hovercraft. Mia was the last one to hug Pablo, but when she got to Spencer, she knew that he wanted to say something to her.

"Yes?" encouraged Mia.

"Here is my e-mail. I wrote it down for you . . . you know, just in case you needed to ask me anything in the future. A question, I mean. You know." Spencer was becoming flustered again and was out of breath. Max knew how hard he tried to remain calm, but he knew Spencer really liked Mia and didn't want her to think of him as a fool.

"Thank you," replied Mia as she took the piece of paper Spencer handed her. "I'll definitely keep in touch." Spencer smiled and relaxed slightly. He couldn't resist raising his hand and placing it on Mia's shoulder. At first he started to pat it. Then he turned his hand to caress her hair, which was back in a braid, the bottom lying near her shoulder blade. It was as soft as a kitten's fur. Mia glanced at her brother, who was having a hard time containing his amusement. Embarrassed at his actions, Spencer withdrew his hand, a blush moving to his cheeks. Feeling sympathetic, Mia stepped forward and patted Spencer on the cheek.

"Good-bye, my friend."

Spencer smiled and raised his hand to his cheek after Mia had withdrawn hers. She turned quickly for the hovercraft. Ben had it ready to go. Once everyone was on board, and their bags were stowed, Ben eased the hovercraft away from the dock and trolled slowly out of the opening into the bigger cave. The engine sounds bounced off the walls, sounding hollow and like a fleet of hovercrafts were leaving. Pablo and Spencer waved good-bye. Soon they moved towards the mouth of the larger cave and onto the ocean. Once there was enough room around them, Ben accelerated, and they were off, skimming lightly and very quickly over the water. Pablo and Spencer were left on the beach, waving as their new friends continued on with their next adventure.

SIX

THE HOVERCRAFT SKIMMED OVER the waves at sixty miles per hour. The pace was steady, and they were making good time. Beside them dolphins jumped in and out of the water trying to keep up with them. Their sleek bodies gleamed as the sun momentarily blazed upon their wet skin. Granny took several pictures. Then the dolphins disappeared, frolicking off somewhere else.

In mere moments, the island shrank into the sea and the banks of angry clouds crowded there. A few hours passed before they saw land again. The closer they came the more wondrous the scenery—a mixture of incredible greens and dark grey rocks. Trees and pastures, cities, and farmland seemed to rise up from the sea.

When they didn't slow, Max was curious as to why. Then he saw a space between two land masses, a bay that seemed to open for them as they arrived. Only with land on both sides of them, did Ben slow his craft.

"Where are you taking us?" asked Max as he moved to stand beside Ben.

"Lisbon. It's tucked inside this bay. This is the mouth of the Rio Tejo."

"The Rio Tejo?" Mia asked.

"Yes, also known as the Tagus River. It's the largest river in Portugal and divides Portugal into two major regions, the mountainous north and the rolling plains of the south."

Max and Mia glanced at each other. If Ben only knew the extensive training they had received, he might not have thought it necessary to explain all this to them.

A little later, they came to a dock where various fishermen's boats were tied up. Ben threw his ropes to a young man on the dock, and he pulled him in.

"Hello, Ben," the young man said. "I'm surprised to see you back so soon. It's only been a day or so since you left."

Once the ropes were secured, Ben urged the Crypto-Capers team to move their things to the dock.

"I wasn't planning on it, Francisco," Ben said to the young man, "but plans do change. We need your help. Do you still have your father's car?"

Francisco, a man with short, chocolate-brown hair neatly combed to the side, had eyes the color of sapphires in the sunlight. His face was soft and round.

"You know I do. I won't give it back to him either until he lays off the Port."

"The Port?" asked Mia as she glanced at Granny.

"Wine, dear. Sounds like Francisco's father has taken too many sips of wine. Portugal is the seventh-largest producer of wine in the world. The most famous is the Vinho do Porto. Also known as simply 'Port.' Your granddad brought me some when he came here years ago on a case. It is quite phenomenal, really, nice tasting and smooth. I haven't had it in years. Your granddad stayed right here in Lisbon—actually . . ." Granny's voice trailed off into her own thoughts.

Max stared at Granny for several seconds as if he were trying to read her mind. He wasn't sure about the change of topic but he agreed with the observation, as well as the resolute manner Francisco had taken in handling his father and his determination to keep him safe.

"Where do you need to go?" asked Francisco.

"The airport, and most urgently," replied Ben.

"You're not coming?" asked Mia curiously.

"I must return to Spencer and Pablo." He then glanced at the menacing clouds rolling in from the west. "And try to beat the storm back to the island. The storm has not arrived there yet, but is still building out over the ocean. I should have time to get back to the island safely. But if I wait much longer, I could be in trouble."

Granny stepped forward. "We appreciate everything you've done, Ben. You've been a great help to us."

"You're certainly welcome, Nellie. May the rest of your journey be safe and prosperous." Ben lavished his charming smile upon the group one last time before turning and hurrying back to his hovercraft.

"Well, let's get a move on," encouraged Francisco. "I should have room for everyone in the truck." Francisco helped grab the Crypto-Capers' luggage and carried it to his truck. It was an old, burnt-red truck, with rust consuming the edges of it. The tailgate was rusted open and could not be closed, looking like it would certainly break off if someone tried. Granny and Francisco loaded into the front of the truck while Emmanuel, Max, and Mia squeezed themselves into positions remotely comfortable in the back. Max, Mia, and Emmanuel glanced one more time at the hovercraft, but with a burst of speed, it skimmed out of the harbor, leaving only the slight wake and swirls of the water caused by its powerful fans.

Francisco headed for the airport. The streets were filled with traffic. As the team glanced around them, they saw rows of houses crunched together with no yards at all. As the afternoon lengthened, streetlamps winked on.

Night was approaching, and, with the storm on its heels, darkness came quickly. Max hoped Ben would make it back to the island safely. For a brief moment he closed his eyes and said a prayer. When he opened them, the truck had turned down a different road, and swung onto another. Before they knew it, they could see the airport. The lights of arriving and departing planes bright in the darkening sky.

"Is there a specific airline you need?"

"Not particularly. Any airline that'll take us to Italy will do," said Granny.

"Well, to be honest, I don't travel often, but I'll drop you off at the front entrance. You can figure it out from there."

"That's just fine. We appreciate the ride, Francisco, and the help," commented Granny.

At the front entrance, Francisco slid into a parking spot. He helped unload their luggage.

"Good luck to you all." Francisco smiled and waved. He hopped back into his truck and drove off. The four of them started grabbing bags until they had them all in hand and carried or rolled them through the sliding automatic doors.

"This way," instructed Granny as she read the signs. As usual, Max surveyed this new terrain. In front of them were the ticket counters for the various airlines, some of which he had heard of before and some he hadn't. He glanced at each person suspiciously, as if waiting for someone to jump out at them, as if the Panther might have guessed this change in plans and preceded them here. He had the strongest feeling that something wasn't right. Then he saw him. A tall thin man in a white airport uniform holding up a sign. Max felt a prickle up his spine when he read the words on the cardboard. "The Crypto-Capers!"

Max called to Mia and Granny and motioned for them to follow. Emmanuel was already in pursuit. When they stood in front of the man, his gaze went from one person to the other as he lowered his sign.

"Excuse me, sir," began Max. "The sign you're holding is for us. We're the Crypto-Capers."

"Your name?" The man inquired firmly as he studied Max apprehensively.

"Max!" The man shook his head, obviously unhappy with the answer.

"Your *full* name."

Max had figured he'd want his full name, but gave only his first to buy time as he assessed the man.

Slowly, Max said, "My full name is Maxwell Sherlock Holmes."

This time, Max's answer seemed to please the man. He looked relieved, though still nervous. Perspiration covered his brow as he reached his hand into his back pocket. His movements were shaky and unsure. Max watched with anticipation, his heart beating vociferously in his chest, sounding like a drum in his ears.

"This is for you. I was instructed to find you and make sure that you receive them." He emptied his palm into Max's hand.

"Thank you." Max's voice was devoid of emotion as he clenched two items in his hand. Before Max could look at what he had received, the man exhaled noisily, then hurried away, disappearing in the crowd.

"What is it?" asked Mia as she peered over her brother's shoulder. Max shook his head as he gazed into his palm. A piece of paper. Something under it felt hard against his skin. As he lifted the folded piece of paper, Max saw a small bronze key. The size of it made Max believe that it should open some kind of lock box. He handed Mia the key, which she placed into her pocket for safe keeping, while he hastily lifted the edges of the folded paper, eager to read it. As he glanced at the message, all eyes seemed to be focused on it.

"What in the world is it?" declared Granny as her hand darted out, seizing the paper. She turned it in one direction, and then the other. For a few minutes, it looked as if she were steering. She stared at the print. Max had seen it and understood her confusion. The words were not jumbled, but they were odd looking. Mia took the paper next. After several seconds of analyzing it, she lowered the paper and smiled.

> GO TO THE LOCKERS ON THE SECOND FLOOR OF THE TERMINAL
> BOX 264

"I know exactly what we need to do."

"What?" Everyone said in unison. The echoing sound caused Mia to quickly glance around her.

"Look at it again," instructed Mia as she raised the paper in front of her. "Do you see anything strange?"

When all they could give her was vacant expressions, Mia exhaled loudly. "Let's go to the loo."

"I don't have to go," said Max. "What I do want to do is figure this out." Admittedly, he was a little put out that his sister had figured out the clue so easily.

"If we go to the loo, we'll figure this out." Mia was again the focus of vacant stares. "Oh, come on!" She turned quickly on her heels and searched the area for the sign to the restrooms. When she found it, she hastily took off in that direction. The group followed.

When they reached the women's restroom, Mia and Granny set down their luggage by the boys.

"We'll be right back." Mia tightly held the paper in her hand at the door. Just inside, she heard Max calling her.

"Mia, wait!" barked Max as he quickly glanced at Emmanuel before joining Mia in the doorway.

"Max, what are you doing?" asked Mia.

"I'm coming with you," he insisted.

"I don't think so. Are you a girl?" The question caused Max's eyebrows to arch.

"No!" he said in a huff. "I'm a man."

Granny placed her hand on Max's shoulder and turned him so he could see the sign.

"This is the women's restrooms, not the men's, dear. You can come in, but I truly don't think you'll be welcomed. Women are funny about things like that." Max stepped back. He hadn't even noticed the signs as he had walked up, his mind was so preoccupied with the note. Again he looked put out.

"Of course!" he said. "Right. So, Emmanuel and I will be watching over the luggage until you return."

Granny smiled and nodded knowingly, then turned and walked into the restroom behind Mia.

The bathroom was immense with cream walls and soft lighting and a long row of stalls. A mural of a Lisbon countryside was painted on the walls in pastel colors. It was most soothing. Several stalls were occupied, and two women stood at the porcelain sinks in front of them, washing their hands and primping themselves in front of the great rectangular mirror. Granny and Mia disappeared into stalls while they waited for the bathroom to clear out.

When it did, Mia stepped out and looked around. She washed and dried her hands. Finished, she raised the paper to the mirror.

"Hey, Granny, look at this!" Granny wasn't there. "Granny?" Then she heard the sound of a toilet flushing, and, a moment later, a stall door opened behind her.

"Yes, dear?" Granny moved to the sinks and washed her hands beside her. Mia was about to say something when she noticed one end of a long piece of toilet paper stuck to the bottom of Granny's shoe. She had made quite a path with it across the bathroom. After showing Granny the note, Mia put it back into her pocket, then bent down and removed the toilet paper from Granny's shoe. She walked around the bathroom swiftly as she wrapped up the toilet paper into one big ball, then threw it into the garbage bin. SCORE!

Mia had to laugh when Granny started fluffing her hair, adjusting the chopsticks that religiously held it in place. She did not realize one bit what Mia had just done. Mia could picture Granny trailing that toilet paper around the terminal unknowingly. That would surely make them easy to follow. Another thought occurred to Mia, and she again took the note from her pocket and put it in front of the mirror.

"Look, Granny! Do you see what I see?"

Granny adjusted her glasses and stared at the mirror, where the words made sense. Granny read them again.

"It doesn't say who sent it," said Granny, "just where to look."

"Right," said Mia. "There has to be more than just this note, doesn't there?"

Granny said, "That's what I think, too."

Mia led the way out of the bathroom.

"What did you find?" asked Max impatiently.

"Follow me and I'll show you," retorted Mia. She grabbed her luggage and led the way to the escalators. Everyone followed, though Max was doing a slow burn that Mia wasn't sharing. When they reached the second floor, Mia looked for the LOCKERS sign. When she found it, she led the way to a tall narrow room with at least a hundred lockers.

"Which one?" asked Emmanuel as he set down the luggage he was holding on the floor.

"Do you know which one?" Max asked Mia, who was heading straight into the room, key in hand. When she stood in front of box 264, she slipped the key into the keyhole, turned it and opened the locker. Inside was another piece of paper. Mia grinned and removed it, opening it so the rest of them could see. It was a cryptogram.

K P S S O G   O G   K O G G O U N !

O   U C C Y   H P T S   V C A Q

V C G   A P G D   O U   Q O G F , O D F A H

V T S S H !

U F D V F U O C A   Z C C Y A C G P K C

"You're up again, Mia," said Max with a touch of frustration.

Mia immediately dropped down to sit on the floor and dug a pencil from her pack. As she began to work, something seemed familiar. She began to fill out the cryptogram and, at the same time, created a cipher key to check out her theory. Sure enough, the cipher key was the same as the one created by the thief when they had solved the case of the missing sock back in Florida.

While he waited for his sister, Max checked the locker to see if there was anything else. Tucked deep in the back was another sheet of paper, instructions and a map of the terminal. A small plane was waiting to take them where they wanted to go.

"Well, we don't have to worry about tickets," he announced. "We're hooked up."

"Yes, I already know that, dear, but by whom?" questioned Granny, her eyebrows arching.

"I can answer that one," started Mia, holding up her pencil. She then proceeded to read the message aloud.

"Who's Nathanial Weedlesome?" asked Emmanuel.

Max sighed. "Morris's father. If he is sending us this cryptogram, then Morris must be in some real trouble."

Max instantly raised his arm and spoke into his watch phone. For several minutes he tried, but there was no answer. "Come on!" urged Max as he rallied everyone, and, following the map, led the team to the airplane that was to take them to Italy.

SEVEN

THE STREET WAS DARK AND OMINOUS as Morris crept down it. Memories of what had happened only a few weeks earlier still clung in his mind. It was like a dream, no, a nightmare. The Panther had come to Pisa, trying to get information from Dante De Luca. Morris hadn't realized how much danger he'd been in at the time. Truthfully, he simply had been in the right place at the precise right time and had acted almost instinctively. His whole being just knew he had to help Dante, as well as help the team. But now, walking that same street and knowing the danger, Morris's courage was fading fast. He focused on Dante's house.

Footsteps! He spun around, his heart pounding, but saw no one after him. He saw instead the Tower of Pisa. Breathing hard, he turned back around to stare at Dante's front door. The house appeared dark. *Dante must be asleep. Why would he request that I visit this late at night and then just go to bed? No, he's in there. Waiting for me.*

Morris was not a brave individual. He knew that. Just going outdoors some days could set off his alarm systems, and, at the moment, every fiber of his being was telling him to run and hide. He was terrified. Even still, he knew he must continue. More than that. He knew he would. Dante had answers they needed to solve the case. He was likely the only one who had some information. Dante alone knew the reasons why all this was happening.

Morris took another step, knees knocking, and pushed himself up the walk. The closer he came to the door, the more Max's words screamed through his mind like an air-raid siren, reminding him in no uncertain terms that he was not to do anything without the team and that he was at that moment ignoring that life-saving advice. And Morris knew Max was right. As a team, he was protected; alone—dog meat.

Morris reached the door. Sweat was pouring off him, and he was puffing like he had just run up a dozen flights of stairs, but he was . . . determined. He reached out to knock, then thought better of it and paused, hand still raised. Out of the corner of his eye he caught the gleam of his watch phone. On the side of it was a button that controlled the sound. For some reason he fixed on it, then pressed the button that would receive waiting calls from Max. He was hoping to hear Max's voice chastising him for what he was doing. *What was he doing?*

Morris hastily lowered his hand and shook his head in frustration, turning to go, feeling both that this was his best course of action and an enormous cop-out. But before he had really turned even part way, Dante's door burst opened, and an elderly, sinewy arm reached out and grabbed Morris by the shoulder of his shirt. That liver-spotted hand had surprising strength. Morris was yanked inside with such force that he was propelled hard into a wall when the hand released him and partially fell. The door was slammed instantly.

Morris's heart raced, and his mind struggled to catch up to what was happening, creating in the meantime a thousand unanswered questions. He tried to see clearly but it was dark in the room, in the whole house. Morris could see nothing.

"Did you come alone?" asked a muffled voice out of the gloom.

"I . . . I . . ." Morris cleared his throat, trying to sound much braver then what he was and utterly failing. "Yes, I came alone," he said firmly. "Could you," and his voice broke, "could you possibly turn on the lights? I'm kinda . . . freaking out here."

"Oh. Sorry about that!" Instantly a lighter flicked into flame in front of Morris's startled eyes. For a moment, that was all he saw, and his eyes focused on that dancing flame as if he had just sprouted moth wings. But then, as his eyes adjusted to the light, he saw the tired features of Dante De Luca highlighted by the lighter.

"Follow me to the kitchen," the old man said. "I have some questions for you."

The man turned and, with the light in front of him, shuffled down a hall. Morris hesitated for a moment before following Dante into the kitchen, but when the light began to fade in the hall, he easily made the choice to gallop after him. Once there, Dante lit several candles on the table. He then put the lighter away and motioned for Morris to sit down.

When he sidled to the chair indicated, Morris saw Dante smile briefly, and his hand went automatically to his hair, trying to smooth down the section of hair that always looked like a cow had come up behind him and licked his hair straight up. Morris adjusted his glasses. Dante looked pale and had dark circles under his eyes, as if he had been stressed for a long time. Morris guessed that Dante had gotten very little sleep of late.

"Um . . . what questions?" Morris asked.

Dante stared at him, even narrowed his eyes a bit. "You are a boy I can trust, yes?"

Morris blinked. "Of course, sir. I'm nothing but loyal—to my friends, that is."

Now Dante really did narrow his eyes to slits. "You're not what you appear to be, boy. You're skinny and sallow and blink a lot. Some would call you . . . what's the word nowadays . . . geeky? A scared little mouse of a kid, but not really. You came. I saw you . . . oh, yes, I saw you a few weeks ago. You were standing behind that tree near the street. And I saw you shoot something into the neck of the intruder harassing me that night. Scared him off. Thank you for that."

Morris said nothing.

"So, who are you really?"

"Well, I guess you could say I am a geek, sir. I am a computer geek and proud of it, too."

Dante began to laugh now, his arms folded over his chest. "That maybe so, but there is more to you than being just a computer geek. You have depth, your will is strong, but beside that you came here with a purpose." Morris began to shake his head. "You did, because I have a feeling you wouldn't have come here otherwise." Morris said nothing, his gaze fixed on Dante. He laughed again. "You can't con a con, son. I know every trick in the book, so don't try to con me."

Morris swallowed hard and cleared his throat. "I'm not trying to con—"

"You know about the tablets don't you?"

Morris gasped. He could feel the blood drain from his face. "Well . . . um . . ."

Dante didn't wait for an answer. "Are you part of the group known as the Crypto-Capers?"

Again Morris gasped, and opened his mouth, but nothing came out for a long moment. Then Morris squeaked, "You want to know the truth?"

Dante looked at Morris sharply. "Why else would I sit in the dark with you?"

Morris said, "Okay, so I really don't know why we're still in the dark. I mean, the shades are all pulled, the curtains all closed, but . . . um, why exactly are we being so secretive?"

Dante unfolded his arms, a look of concern came on his candle-lit face. "I don't want anyone to know I'm home, or that you're here. Look, boy, just answer the questions."

Morris had stalled for time, trying to figure out what he should do. Nothing much had come to him. *Straight truth then*, he thought. "Yes, I'm one of the Crypto-Capers, and yes, I do know about the tablets, but you might not know that the rest of my team is on their way here with your grandson, Emmanuel. They're already enroute. *And*, we have the tablet of the Jaguar *and* a sundial in our possession."

Dante raised his hand to his lips, his eyes wide and bulging. "How could . . . when did . . . you are?" Dante stuttered. He then breathed deeply, trying to overcome his surprise. "I'm impressed. Truly, I am. Men much older and more experienced then you could not accomplish what your team has in such a short period of time." Dante breathed deeply again. "But you never should have gotten Emmanuel involved in this. He is a good boy, and strong, and he's spent years protecting the sundial, but you've put him in great danger."

"I'm afraid danger was finding him ahead of us. We thought he would be safer with us," said Morris. "You must know that Emmanuel was trying to protect the sundial . . . and you, and he still is. My team and I are determined to solve the Legend of the Golden Monkey. Not for our own gain, for we don't seek glory or riches, but to protect it from the one man who would be selfish enough to destroy anyone in his way just to get his hands on it. We saved Emmanuel from the wrath of the Panther. And it was the Panther who visited you the day we met. And he's after my team and Emmanuel to get his hands on the tablet of the Jaguar and the sundial. He is after the other pieces as well."

Dante sat back in his chair, seeming to have suddenly gone weak.

"So again, Dante, your life is in danger."

The old man nodded, as if he had come to this conclusion on his own.

Morris leaned toward him. "The Crypto-Capers can help. Trust us. Tell me the location of the other pieces. We need to get that Golden Monkey before the Panther does. It's imperative."

Dante stared at Morris, shaking his head. He sighed. "You don't understand, boy. Many years ago my brother and I opened the treasure room at Chichen Itza. We put all the pieces together and opened the room. But . . . there was nothing in it. The Golden Monkey does *not* exist." Dante covered his eyes with his aging hands. "I can't help you."

"There's a false room."

Dante removed his hands from his face and stared hard at Morris. "A false room? A false room!" For a moment Morris could almost see the man's mind race. "No. No. That can't be. How do you know?"

"I'm surprised you didn't know."

Dante's gaze went unfocused as memories of another time in his life filled him. Morris could see shame in his face as those memories forced their way through his mind.

Gently, Morris said, "Your brother, Marcello, was desperate to open the treasure room, wasn't he? You wanted to do more research at Machu Picchu before you did. You had an instinct, Dante, a gut feeling that drove you that day. You knew something wasn't right when you opened the treasure room for the first time, didn't you?"

Dante pressed his eyes shut.

"You knew something was missing!"

"No! I mean—yes!" Dante eyes were filled with sadness and remorse. "It was . . . too easy. Everything fit, but it was wrong. How do you know this?"

"My team and I analyzed the wall at the Carocal. You need four pieces, not three, to open the treasure room. The two tablets, one of the eagle and one of the jaguar, and *two* sundials. Emmanuel has one, and we found the tablet of the jaguar. We need the other sundial and the tablet of the eagle. I'm thinking you know where they are."

Dante shook his head forcefully. "I know where the other tablet is, and Emmanuel's been keeping my sundial safe, but I don't know about another sundial."

"Then that's where you went wrong. Think, Dante. Remember all that you can. You know where the other sundial is."

Dante slowly shook his head. "I honestly don't." He suddenly looked years older and tired. He scraped his chair back from the table and walked into his living room, pausing to gaze up at the painting of the Chechen tree. "When my brother and wife had passed, I was truly lost for a long time. Out of my mind. When I returned from Chichen Itza, I had to bury them. It was the hardest thing

I ever had to do in my life. I went to my brother's apartment a few months after the funeral. I know it sounds weak, but I couldn't breathe in the air where my brother once had. It was too painful, still too fresh.

"When I opened the door, I saw that his apartment had been torn apart. Someone had had been looking for something. I thought it must be the tablets, but by that time I had already hidden them and my sundial to keep them as far away from my mind as possible. I sold off or got rid of most of my brother's belongings. A few things I kept. Sentimental value. Some are here around the house, decorations, and some I put away." As Dante spoke he moved towards something on the table near the wall. Morris stood to see what it was.

"That's a pretty box. What's in it?" asked Morris.

Dante shrugged. "It's a cryptex."

Morris's eyes popped open. "You're joking! I've never seen one before. Heard about them, of course, but seen one up close—no." Enthusiasm filled Morris.

"Well, this cryptex is not like ones you may have heard or read about. This one has a four-number password, not five letters. Because of its uniqueness, it must have been specially made for my brother. The problem is, I don't know the combination. This minor problem keeps it as decoration and nothing more."

The cryptex needed a *four-number* combination. Excitement tickled at Morris's mind. Before he could say anything, though, both he and Dante froze. Someone was jostling the handle on the front door.

Morris's heartbeat instantly began to race. Dante grabbed him by the front of his grey coveralls and half dragged him into another room, shoving him into a dark clothes closet. Dante pushed inside as well, and Morris felt a hanger dig into his back.

"They've come for me, Morris," whispered Dante, his eye looking out a crack in the mostly closed door. Morris had a more obstructed view, but, being shorter than Dante, did get a glimpse of the room, a spare bedroom, he thought. On the wall, above a tile fireplace opposite him, Morris saw a painting he was sure he had seen somewhere before.

"Who's come for you?" Morris whispered and loosened his collar as the first waves of claustrophobia started to affect him.

"Men who wish to keep me quiet, boy."

"Mr. De Luca—Dante, please, let me out of here. I . . ." Morris tried to squeeze past Dante, but the man held him tight.

"Listen, boy, we might only have a few seconds before the house is taken, and us with it. I need to disappear for a while."

Morris began to shake his head, but Dante grabbed his jaw. "Look at me. You're the brightest person I've ever met, so I know that you'll understand what I have to do and why you can't come with me. Do what you've come here to do. Solve your case. Find the Golden Monkey. You and your team have already done well, discovered much. What I have in this house alone should help you find success."

"What of Emmanuel, Dante? You can't disappear
. . . he needs you."

Dante removed his hand from Morris's face, his
head dropping to his chest. "I can't protect him anymore.
You brought him to the lion's den." Then even in the darkness, Morris could see Dante's eyes glint as he looked out
again. "Emmanuel knows more than he thinks. A sponge,
that boy is. He should be invaluable to you." Then Dante
gripped Morris's shirt, pulling him to within an inch of his
face. "Promise me, boy . . . promise me you'll protect him."
The moment was broken with the sound of glass breaking.
"Promise me!"

"I promise!"

Dante patted Morris's cheek, then shoved him
hard to the back of the closet.

"Don't come out while they're in the house. You'll
be safe here." With that, the door swung open, then
closed. Morris heard the sound of retreating footsteps,
then the grinding of stone. There was a moment of
silence, then he heard loud steps running from the other
side of the house. Morris could tell the intruders were
male; they made no pretense of lowering their voices as
they spoke. Morris could hear everything being said.

"Where is he? Did you see him?" asked one of the
men, who Morris figured was in his late teens.

"No! I could've sworn I heard something over
here, but now . . . isn't there one light in this house that
works?" The men searched the house, not bothering to
check the closet of the spare bedroom Morris was in.

People generally kept spare bedrooms rather pristine and empty. He guessed the intruders believed that too. They tore the rest of the house apart, though. Morris heard loud crashes of overturned desks and hutches and breaking glass and ceramic. He heard the scrape and thud of heavy furniture being moved. Someone came into the spare bedroom and poked around, then left. After an hour or so, Morris heard a door slam. Then came quiet.

Fear helped keep Morris in the back of the dark closet. He ignored his claustrophobia, trying to overcome it, but it was difficult. He wanted to scream and rush out of the room, but common sense stopped him. Upon hearing silence for at least half an hour, Morris felt it was safe to leave the closet.

In the dark, he inched quietly to the door, felt for the door handle. A ray of moonlight through the keyhole glinted off his watch. Not wanting to be caught with it and having enemies use it for their own gain, Morris removed the watch and tucked it into his front tool pocket. Then he reached again for the door handle.

After taking a deep breath to calm his nerves, Morris slowly gripped the handle and turned it. The soft *click* the latch made sounded very loud in the quiet, causing Morris to pause several seconds. When no sound responded, Morris pushed the door open, cringing at the creaking of the hinges and stepped out. Again he waited to see if anyone heard. Nothing. He stepped cautiously into the hallway, his eyes searching the dark for the intruders. He sighed, relieved that he was safe.

Something heavy slammed against his back, and Morris fell to the floor in a heap. He partially rolled over, his hair over part of his face. Fortunately, his glasses had stayed in place. A light came on, something like a camp lantern, Morris thought. As he blinked to adjust to the sudden light and to keep from losing conscientiousness, someone leaning over him, glancing at pictures in his hand. The man's skin was tan, and he was wearing a black leather jacket. What made him stand out was his spiky yellow hair with red tips.

"Who do you think this is, Theryn?" another voice said from someplace near him. "Should we take him with us?" The intruders hadn't left. They had stayed in the house . . . waiting for something? Him? Morris silently cursed himself for his mistake. Max wouldn't have been so easily duped.

"Naw, Willard. Leave him. He's not in any of the photos, so I don't think he's important. Look at him. Grey coveralls? A uniform? He is some kind of repairman. Probably making a service call to fix the lights."

Morris had put on the grey coveralls because he had been visiting customers for his dad all day. It was appropriate attire for the work.

"This late?" the man call Willard questioned.

Theryn shrugged, not wanting to analyze it.

"I don't know the hours of those people. All I know is what we're told. And we were told to stop the people in these pictures." Theryn held up the pictures to his friend and smacked them with the back of his hand.

At that point, Morris caught a glimpse of the snapshots. They were of Max, Mia, Pablo, Spencer, Granny, and Emmanuel.

"Yeah, but didn't the boss say their plane had exploded?" asked Willard.

"Yeah, he did, but I got the impression he didn't think that would kill them, only delay them, you fool. Boss needs the artifacts they carry. Why would he destroy them and drop them in the ocean if he needed stuff they had?"

"Oh."

"These people are brilliant. They probably could find a way out of that situation." He chuckled darkly. "But they don't know about us. We're the Panther's insurance policy. We need to get him the things he needs. Get it? If we do a good job, he might allow us to do other jobs for him and get more money. Remember the money. Panther pays very well." Theryn stepped around Morris, tucking the pictures neatly in his shirt pocket.

"So, the Panther's gonna come here if we get the stuff he wants?"

"Come here? Are you nuts? No, we need to get back to him with the artifacts. Now, let's dash. We can leave this dumb service guy here. By the time he comes to, we'll be long gone."

With that, Theryn and Willard walked out of the house, leaving Morris on the floor.

EIGHT

MAX WAS IN AN INTERESTING predicament. He was in the bathroom on the airplane. They were only twenty minutes out from the approach to the airport, when he got the notion to try Morris again. He had been debating on it for some time, knowing that he probably wouldn't answer. But never giving up hope, he raised his watch closer to his mouth, not wanting to shout and have everyone overhear him through the door. That's when he heard something. He turned up the volume on his watch and placed it closer to his ear.

He was overhearing a conversation. Between who, he wasn't sure, then he overheard a name. Theryn. Who was Theryn? As the dialogue continued, Max's mouth opened wider. A man identified as Willard was speaking too, and from what these two men said, they were accomplices of the Panther, and they were looking for the Crypto-Capers team. Max waited until the conversation was over before he rushed out of the bathroom, almost taking out a stewardess standing just outside. Then he heard the pilot tell the passengers they would be landing shortly, his voice calm over the speakers.

Max hurried to his seat across from Mia. Their plane was similar to Pablo's, except bigger. The seats were a soft, cushy leather, and they had all relaxed, no longer falling out of the sky or hiking for miles. Mia had been reading a magazine when he plopped down in his seat. She glanced at him, then back at the page she had been reading, then sharply up at him again.

"Max, what's wrong?" Mia let the magazine slip from her lap as she leaned toward him. "Max?"

Max turned towards Granny, who was snoring loudly in the seat next to him. His gaze then slipped past Mia to Emmanuel, who was sleeping but tossing his head from side to side as if in a bad dream. Then he leaned close to Mia. "Morris is in trouble."

Mia scrunched up her face. "We know that, silly, remember? That's why we're on this plane," Mia's tone was soft and relaxed.

"No, Mia. I just heard something quite disturbing." Max wetted his lips with his tongue. "We have some new players in the game. Apparently, the Panther sent two more men after us . . . only right now they're ahead of us. One's name is Theryn. The other is Willard. They're looking for us. They know we have the two artifacts in our possession, and the Panther wants them. They also know the bomb on the plane only delayed us."

Mia raised her right hand to cover her mouth. "They have Morris, don't they?"

Max grunted loudly and shook his head. "Actually, no. Morris's anonymity was his saving grace.

The Panther might know we have another team member, but he doesn't know what he looks like. The men left Morris lying somewhere. He might be hurt. My guess is that Morris didn't follow my advice and went to see Dante on his own."

"What?" Emmanuel had woken abruptly from his sleep. "What did you say?" he asked sleepily.

Max took a deep breath and steadied his gaze on Emmanuel. "I think Morris went to your grandfather's house looking for him."

When Max didn't continue, Emmanuel blurted, "And?"

Max ran a hand through his hair. "And that's it. That's all I know. I overheard a conversation through my watch phone. The only way I'd be able to do that is if Morris had somehow leaned on the connect button, which means he knew he was in danger."

"Morris spoke with my grandfather once, so he is probably with him." A sparkle instantly shone in Emmanuel's eyes. "Or, my grandfather went into hiding again."

"Again?" asked Mia.

"Grandfather has a habit of hiding when situations get rough."

Max raised his fingers to tap his chin in thought. "Where's his hiding spot?"

"If I knew that, then it wouldn't be a hiding spot, would it?"

"You have a point, but surely you must know some place he favors."

69

Emmanuel thought for a moment, then shook his head. "He *likes* many places, but none of them would be good hiding spots."

"Hmmmmm," Max crooned loudly. "I've got it! I bet Morris and your grandfather were talking when the two men broke up the conversation."

"That would be logical," said Mia.

"If Emmanuel's right," Max continued, "and his grandfather ran, that means Morris was left behind."

"Yeah, but where?" asked Mia.

Max's mind filled with possibilities. Then it hit him. They had an easy way to determine Morris's location. Why hadn't he thought about it before?

"Mia, where's the cell phone?"

Mia pointed behind him. "Oh, it is in Granny's handbag. I saw her check the battery on it earlier."

Granny's handbag! Max was loathe to look inside the brightly colored, shapeless leather mass. The only thing that differentiated it from an artist's painting was the leather strap . . . and the amount of junk it held. Granny carried the handbag everywhere and put—who knows what—in it. She had a propensity of pulling odd things out of it. Max eyed the handbag by Granny's feet.

"Go on!" encouraged Mia with a sly grin.

Max turned and glared at his sister. "Can't you do it? Going into another woman's handbag is . . . more of a girl thing, isn't it?"

Emmanuel chuckled, but he immediately choked it off when Mia's narrow gaze centered on him.

"You want the cell?" Mia said. "Then you can get it. I refuse to touch Granny's handbag. The last time I opened it to get something out, I could have sworn something moved inside it." Mia shuddered and sat back in her seat, folding her arms over her chest, a determined expression upon her face.

Max began to stand up, then he sat back down. He tried to reach for the handbag but quickly retracted his hand.

Mia let out an exasperated sigh. "Oh, you big baby. Just wake her up and *ask* her. I mean . . . *honestly!*"

Max glared at his sister before resting a hand on Granny's arm. "Granny? Granny, are you awake?"

Granny woke instantly and immediately ran her fingers over her hair. "Are we there yet?"

"We should be landing shortly. Um . . . Granny, can I see the cell phone for a minute?"

"Sure, dear. I have it right here in my handbag. You could have just gotten it yourself. I wouldn't have minded." Granny leaned forward and grabbed hold of her handbag, needing a good grip to hoist it into her lap. She opened it and plunged her right hand inside, sweeping back and forth, looking for the cell phone. "I know it's in here somewhere." She then grabbed the opening of her bag and pulled it up to her face. "Oh, rubbish! Here, hold this for me, won't you dear?"

Granny took out a ball of yellow yarn and plopped it down into Max's outstretched hands. She then took out a wad of zip ties, a solid red brick, a lock-picking kit, two flashlights, a manicure set, what looked suspiciously like a stick of dynamite, a foot-long file, one fuzzy pink slipper, and four hairpins. Max had no idea how all this stuff had fit in the handbag.

Granny was so consumed with her search that she didn't see the surprised looks on Max and Mia's faces, their jaws dropping in surprise. Granny was a very unique woman, and though Max and Mia thought they were used to her eccentric ways, they were still surprised by some of the things she did. There really just wasn't any explanation for what she kept in her handbag.

His arms full, Max hoped Granny would find the phone soon. Then he felt something in his arms move, and a tail whipped out and was gone so fast he wasn't sure it was rodent or lizard. "Ah, Granny—"

"Oh—here it is!" Granny smiled broadly as she lifted the phone in the air. Their cell was a bright candy apple-red, and could do amazing things. Besides the fact that the phone contained an electric charge, as well as steal cable for emergency situations, it could also do several other things. What interested Max was its GPS tracking feature. Morris had given it to them after their case in Las Vegas when Mia was kidnapped, replacing their older phone.

Granny tucked the phone into her hair and started taking back all the stuff she had dumped into Max's arms. "Ah, Granny," Max said, "I think there's something living in there."

"Don't be ridiculous," Granny said, but she peeked into the pink slipper and smiled before she returned it to the handbag. With everything stowed again, she pulled the phone from her hair and handed it to Max.

Max turned on the phone. Each of them had a password and a nickname associated with their location, including Morris. Each of them had a GPS chip in their shoulders, and Morris was no exception. Max went to work, typing in Morris's password and nickname. It made him chuckle when he typed in, "thief hunter." Instantly a map came up. A dot slowly came into focus and began blinking. He was in Pisa, Italy. Max immediately turned the phone for Emmanuel to see.

"Does this location look familiar?"

Emmanuel took the cell phone and gazed closer at the screen. He then turned his gaze away.

"What is it?" asked Mia.

"That's Grandfather's house."

Before any more could be said, they were landing. Emmanuel returned the phone to Max, who put it in his backpack. The plane taxied to the terminal, and the group grabbed all of their belongings and made their way through the airport. Once they reached the outer doors where cars parked to load and unload passengers, they saw someone waiting for them. It was Nathanial Weedlesome, Morris's dad.

NINE

MR. WEEDLESOME PACKED everyone's belongings into a van while the group loaded inside. When he had moved into traffic, he said, "Tell me what is going on, Maxwell."

Mr. Weedlesome looked as if he hadn't slept. His eyes were red and puffy. His salt-and-pepper hair was thin and lanky like Morris's, with a similar upright section in the back. Square black spectacles rode low on his nose, and though his appearance emanated exhaustion, he still appeared intelligent. Mr. Weedlesome was a very smart man, which explained Morris's genius.

"What's happened, Mr. Weedlesome?" asked Mia softly.

Mr. Weedlesome tightened his grip on the steering wheel before answering. "The office sent me here to work on a company's computer hardware. That's classified." Mr. Weedlesome said curtly. "As you know, when I make trips, I often set up visits to homes and help old customers with their computer issues. Morris comes with me on occasion. He had several service calls today, but he hasn't returned. I've been trying to get hold of him through his cell, but he won't answer."

"Do you have a list of the customers he saw today?" asked Max.

"Of course! I've been driving around for the past few hours checking each location, but he wasn't at any of them. Each customer said that Morris arrived promptly for the appointment, and when finished, he called a cab or walked. I went back to the hotel to wait, but still nothing. I need answers, Max, and I know you have them."

Streetlights illuminated the street, but the sky was dark and cloudy. Granny sat in the front passenger seat and glanced at Max, sitting in one of the back seats.

"We know where Morris is, Mr. Weedlesome."

The van screeched to a stop, jolting everyone.

"Where!" barked Mr. Weedlesome.

"For heaven's sake, Nathan, you can't just stop in the middle of traffic," scolded Granny, fixing her hair.

Mr. Weedlesome blinked and stepped on the gas again. "Where?" asked Mr. Weedlesome again, his tone more controlled and calm.

"He's at my grandfather's house," said Emmanuel, "Dante De Luca's house here in Pisa."

Mr. Weedlesome frowned. "What's he doing there?"

"Looking for information," replied Emmanuel.

Mr. Weedlesome glanced in his rearview mirror at Emmanuel but said nothing. After several deep breaths, Mr. Weedlesome said, "Tell me where I need to go."

Max pulled out the cell phone, turned on the GPS, and with Emmanuel's help, guided Mr. Weedlesome to Dante De Luca's townhouse.

75

Before he let anyone out of the van, Max studied the house and their surroundings. The streetlights shone brightly. He saw shiny flecks of light all over Dante's porch. Max knew this was caused by broken glass. Even in the dark it was easy to see that the front door was slightly ajar. It looked like someone had forced it. Max grabbed his backpack and opened the van door. Mia followed quickly behind. When Emmanuel rose from his seat, Max stopped him.

"We don't know what we'll find, Emmanuel. Stay here until we call for you."

Mr. Weedlesome opened his door, but Max quickly closed it, too. "Granny!" Max didn't wait to hear her reasons why Mr. Weedlesome shouldn't come. She then stepped out of the van and quickly followed behind her grandchildren, leaving Mr. Weedlesome and Emmanuel looking after them from the safety of the van.

Max glanced at the phone and could see the dot that was Morris blinking faster. He knew that Morris was inside, not moving, so possibly tied up or injured. Up on the porch, he rested his hand on the door and pushed it open slowly. It squeaked loudly, which sent a shiver down his spine. Mia entered right behind him.

Inside was dark. Max couldn't see a thing. He hastily retrieved a flashlight from his backpack. As they stepped further into the vestibule, a soft light focused their attention to the right. "This way!" Max whispered.

Granny held her flashlight like a club, ready to use it as a weapon if necessary.

In the kitchen they found several lit candles. Strings of wax had dribbled down the sides and pooled in the holders, indicating that the candles had been burning for some time, but lit by whom?

Max's steps were soft and measured as he moved slowly into the kitchen. Once inside, he spotted Morris. He was lying on the floor in a heap. His long hair half covering his face. Before Max could stop her, Mia ran to him, dropping to her knees by his side.

"Morris? Morris!" shouted Mia as she shook his shoulder. When he didn't move, Mia pushed his hair from his face. She then placed her hand above his mouth. She could feel the warmth of his breath upon her skin. "He's breathing!"

Max and Granny dropped to their knees. Granny dug some smelling salts from her handbag and waved it in front of his nose. Morris shot up so fast that Max and Mia fell on their backsides in shock.

"Wha-what happened?" Morris sputtered. He rubbed his neck. As his eyes began to focus he realized that his team was around him. "Max! Mia! Granny!" A smile rose to Morris's lips. "I'm so glad you're here."

Max stood and helped Morris to his feet.

"We're glad you're okay, mate," said Max as he patted Morris on the arm. "You had us worried."

Mia hugged him. "We used the GPS to find you!"

Morris wrapped his arms around Mia. Then Granny embraced him so tightly he was gasping for air. When she released him, he was no longer so pale.

"Sorry, dear," Granny said, "but you gave us quite a scare. Your father's sitting in a van outside waiting for us. He's worried to death."

Morris's hand rose to his forehead. "Is he angry?"

"He's more concerned. You didn't tell him where you were going, dear," scolded Granny.

"*And* you didn't wait for us," added Max sternly.

"I know, Max. I know I should've waited, but Dante asked me to come. I couldn't refuse him. We need his help. And I found out some things that can help us. Dante told me he wasn't aware of another sundial. He also said that the answers are in this house somewhere."

Max's forehead furrowed.

Morris then added hopefully, "Did you, by chance, overhear the Panther's accomplices' conversation?"

Max grinned. "Every word. That was brilliant."

"I only heard part of it, myself, but what I did hear and saw makes me certain that those men were after Dante. But not just him, they were after all of us, too."

"Where's Dante?" asked Granny.

"I don't know. Before he left, he shoved me into a closet and told me to stay there. He said he had to leave, that he must not be caught. I have no idea where he went. All I know was that he barely escaped because as soon as he left, I heard glass break and the front door open."

Granny looked around them. "They tore this place up, didn't they?"

"Yeah. I'm scared they found the clues we need, but they didn't seem particularly bright. They might have

missed the important stuff. Let's fan out and start looking."

"What kinds of things?" asked Mia.

"I don't know. Dante never said what they were."

The team immediately split up and searched the
house, each of them taking a room. They searched through
the kitchen and the bathrooms, the closets and Dante's
bedroom upstairs. His townhouse wasn't terribly huge and
within an hour they had searched almost every crevice.
While the team was searching, Granny noticed something
odd sitting on the mantle of the fireplace in the spare bedroom on the first floor. It was a statue of the Tower of Pisa,
above that was a painting with wondrous swirls and depth.
Amid all of the thick dust covering everything else on the
mantle, including the picture frames, the statue was the
only item without a speck of dust. Granny wrapped her
hand around it, but, when she tried to lift it, for some reason, it wouldn't come up. But it did move. She heard a soft
click, and the fireplace began to rotate. Granny barely had
time to step out of the way.

As Granny watched the fireplace return to its
original orientation, she saw again the statue of the
Tower of Pisa. This must have been how Dante had
escaped. About then, Morris came into the room with a
flashlight and paused. He went to the closet and opened
the door. "This is odd," he said.

"What's odd, dear?" asked Granny.

Morris said, "Well, something's wrong. There
aren't any clothes in this closet. No hangers. One poked

me in the back when Dante shoved me into it. And . . . well it's weird, but the closet should be over there," he said pointing to a space of blank wall.

Granny went to the wall and ran her hand down and across it, tapping. She smiled. Then she pushed at a section of wall, and . . . it opened.

Morris's jaw dropped. From the inside, he hadn't been able to tell that it was a secret closet. That was why the thugs never opened it and Dante had said he'd be safe. He picked up the cryptex that Dante had left there.

Granny shone her light around the closet, looking around. She immediately dropped to her knees. Dust bunnies and cobwebs littered the floor. Granny was about to rise, not seeing much of anything that could help them, when she noticed a box. Granny took it out and opened it. Inside were several photo albums, picture frames, memento kinds of things, a guidebook, a flyer with information about the Camposanto Monumentale, and an old weathered journal.

Granny lifted out the guidebook, the Camposanto Monumentale flyer, and the journal. She looked at the journal first. Granny rubbed her thumb across the bottom, over the letters, "M.D."

"Marcello De Luca!" whispered Granny, and Morris smiled. She picked up the items she had selected and left the box in the secret closet. The rest of the team had congregated in the living room.

"Find anything?" Granny asked the others.

"Not a thing!" replied Max.

"I found something," said Mia, "but I'm not sure if it's important. I found a business card with a name on it." Mia held up the card between her fingers.

"Whose?" asked Max. Mia glanced at the card.

"'Liliana Staletti—tour guide of the Italian monuments.' I found it stuck in the corner of a mirror."

"Granny?" asked Max.

She smiled with just a touch of smugness. "Three things that hold importance, I'm sure." Granny showed the team what she had. They glanced at the items in curiosity. Max touched the edge of the journal cover and lifted it. He instantly saw a name he recognized. The rest of the words were written in English and Italian.

"We'll take these with us to look over more closely. Every second we remain here I feel we're in danger. Morris, did you find anything?"

As Max spoke, Morris held out the small wooden box. He then glanced up at the Chechen tree hanging on the wall. Max joined him, as did Mia and Granny.

"Is it just me, or does this remind us of a story?" offered Max.

"The Tale of the Two Brothers," inserted Mia.

"Exactly!" said Granny. "What's inside the box, Morris?"

"A cryptex!" Morris said. The box was six inches in length and made out of rosewood. It had a gold clasp. "When I was talking to Dante, he told me that this cryptex was his brother's. The box was specially made for him. He must have taken it into the closet with us."

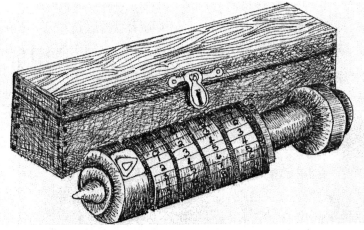

"And what do you think is inside?" asked Granny. "Did he mention that?"

Without turning his head, Morris smiled knowingly. "He revealed much more than he wanted, I think. Dante claimed he knew nothing about a second sundial, which we figured existed because of the treasure room in the Carocal. However, there's no way a sundial would be set in the treasure room. There's no light down there."

"No, it was almost completely dark," said Mia. "You know, I've been thinking about that. We have Emmanuel's sundial and the copy I bought just in case. Maybe the sundial is for the *top* of the ruin, to be placed towards the rising of the sun. That makes sense doesn't it?"

"More than you know," said Morris in admiration.

"Then what would go in the treasure room?" asked Granny, slightly confused.

Mia said, "I'm thinking, a piece the same size as the sundial, something to link the two tablets together to form one big piece. This big piece would open the treasure room. It is just a theory, but a logical one."

Suddenly, Morris snapped his finger, and his eyes lit up. "Dante lied to me," he said. "He *had* to know there was another object. I believe he and Marcello placed the sundial in the wrong position. That's why it opened a false treasure room. That's why Dante wanted to go to Machu Picchu—to see the ruins there and to see the still-intact sundial. He needed a better idea of where to place it. Marcello had been in a hurry, though, and wanted the treasure more than he wanted the correct information. Yes, that must've been it. That makes complete sense."

It did make sense and somehow answered many questions. "The resentment Marcello must have felt was because he knew his brother had been correct, and he cursed his own impatience."

"But that missing piece can't be inside the cryptex, can it?" asked Granny.

Morris said, "No, but what could be is a *clue* to find the other piece, or maybe a clue to lead us someplace else or to something else. I really don't know, but I do have an idea of the combination."

Morris set the box on the table and opened it. Inside was a beautifully detailed cryptex. The ends were made of pure gold and the middle had four pearl-shaped rings with numbers on them. The numbers were large and appeared to go up to twenty.

"How in the world are we going to be able to open that?" asked Mia.

"What do you mean?" said Morris. "We already know the combination."

TEN

MAX GLANCED AT MORRIS, then at Mia and Granny. He smiled, knowing already what Morris had meant. "If you recall, we found Mayan numbers at the Carocal in the treasure room scratched into the stone by one of the tablet impressions. I'll bet those numbers will open the cryptex. Mia, did you write those numbers down?"

"Yes! They were Fibonacci numbers."

Mia pulled out her notepad and flipped the pages until she reached what she was looking for. "Here it is. The numbers were simple and straight forward. Though we could have created a math problem with them, we found, by using a base twenty system—because of the way they were etched into the stone—we didn't have to. There was no indication for us to make the answer more complicated than what it was. All we had to do was find out what the numbers were. No multiplying, adding together, or anything needed to be done.

_____and_____

(Refer back to Book 3 for the answers and write them down.)

Mia said the numbers out loud, then said, "The problem is, there are only three digits, but, obviously, here we need four.

"Correct," answered Morris. "Which is why we need to add a zero in front of the single digit. So the numbers should look like this as they are broken apart in order." Morris wrote down the order on Mia's notepad so they had it for reference.

_____   _____   _____   _____

"Are you sure?" asked Granny. "We only have one chance at this, don't we? The message in the cryptex will be ruined if we input the wrong numbers."

"Yeah. Just one chance," replied Morris as he took a deep breath and lifted out the cryptex. "But, Granny, I'm positive I'm correct."

"Then go ahead, dear." Granny placed an encouraging hand upon his shoulder and squeezed. Morris absorbed her courage like a sponge and turned the dials carefully to the numbers on the paper. Morris exhaled a breath of relief when he heard a soft *click* but not the breaking of glass that spelled ruin.

"By all means, boy, open it."

Morris's hand froze in the act of opening the cryptex. The speaker was not a member of his team.

Granny turned first, then Mia and Max. Morris was the last. When he turned he saw the teen with spiky yellow hair with red tips. His leather jacket was sleek and shiny. Another teen was standing next to him. Both were grinning.

"Williard and Theryn, I presume?" said Max confidently. He had carefully placed himself between the intruders and Morris, the least experienced team member.

Theryn performed an elaborate but mocking bow. "At your service. You and your team just saved us some work. Now, if you don't mind, hand over the cryptex and everything else you found. The Panther will be pleased." Then he began to laugh menacingly. The sound of it echoed throughout the house.

"What is your problem?" snarled Mia, who also shielded Morris.

"My problem? Nothing! I laugh because the Panther's a genius. He said for us to wait until *you* found what we needed. I had no idea you guys would even come here. He knew, though. I almost doubted him, but sure enough, here you are, and you found stuff the Panther needs. Now, hand me the cryptex and the other stuff, and be quick about it."

Granny turned to Morris and gave him a penetrating stare. She saw the turn of his head and slight nod. Morris handed her the cryptex as his thumb grazed one of the numbers, moving it. She then took the journal, the guide book, and the Composanto information from Max, as well as the card from Mia and placed it inside of the journal for safe keeping. But, instead of handing everything over, Granny held all the items to her chest. "Boys, take this if you must, but what's here is beyond your comprehension." Granny seemed about to step forward, but then reconsidered. Instead, she tutted her tongue in obvious disdain at Williard and Theryn.

"I bet you two don't know exactly what the Panther's looking for, do you? Nor what we found."

The smile on Theryn's face faltered slightly. Before he could speak, Willard's voice rang out. "Of course, we know. Would we be here if we didn't?"

"I believe you'd go anywhere the money's good, more than happy to follow the Panther to glory and riches. Am I right?"

Willard glanced at Theryn, but Theryn only glared at Granny as she continued with her assessment.

"You're two gits on a fool's errand. Do you honestly believe that we're just going to turn over what we found to you? Are you mental?"

Morris, Max, and Mia all glanced in amazement at Granny. She stood a foot in front of them all, almost daring Theryn and Willard to hurt them. She seemed to be looking for a fight.

"Granny, what are you doing?" whispered Max. "Stop antagonizing them."

"Let her!" murmured Morris as his attention on the accomplices remained unwavering.

Max glanced at Morris, and was about to retort, when Theryn spoke. "So you think we won't hurt you, old lady? Believe me, we could. We don't want it to come down to that, but we can get pretty nasty."

"You're two against four. I dare you to try."

"Actually, it's three against your four. Do you honestly think these two idiots are here alone?" The voice came from the vestibule. The man came slowly and deliberately into the room. All eyes were on him. When he moved into the light, Max's jaw dropped slightly. Mia took a quick intake of breath. Morris shook his head in disbelief. Granny spoke what everyone was thinking? "You? It can't be. You're in a Florida jail."

The man laughed softly and yet the sound was harsh and evil. "I *was* in a prison, actually a *high security* prison. I got moved there when the judge found out I was the notorious Panther's son. I wonder who had a hand in that? Hmm?" Denton Miles glared at the Crypto-Capers. Then he focused mostly on Morris. "It doesn't matter though, because I was able to get out. In all honesty, it's amazing what fathers can do, and mine has a pretty wide reach." Denton stretched his arms to either side and flexed his hands in meaning.

It had been months since their first case in the United States when Denton had stolen the famous antique sock from Mr. Delacomb that contained a pair of diamond-studded Prada sunglasses. Denton's appearance had definitely changed since those days. Still tall and lanky, his previously long blonde hair had been cropped close to his ears. Before, they could barely see the color of his eyes, but now the cold blueness of them glistened like ice.

"Now, unlike my companions, I *do* know what my father is after, and while I have you in my grasp, I also want the sundial and the tablets you found in Chichen Itza."

The Crypto-Capers expressions were opaque, no one giving anything away.

It caused Denton to smile. "So, Nellie, the lives of your team, your grandchildren . . . or the valuables?"

As Granny's gaze focused on Denton, his hand patted the chest of his jacket, indicating that he had a weapon. She stared at his face, but his features were reserved and hardened. Gone was the college student trying to make an extra buck. This was a cold, unrelenting man looking to become the next Panther.

Granny said, "You know I can't, and will not, do that. You're going down the wrong path, Denton. Reconsider, I beg you. You go down this road and there's no turning back. You're becoming your father. Do you really want to be on the run all the time, half the world on your heels? That will be your fate."

Denton was unmoved by the speech. "Theryn!" was all that he said. Granny took a deep breath. Theryn took a threatening step forward, pulling out a small lead pipe from the inside of his leather jacket and thumping the end several times in his hand. Willard grabbed a nearby metal candlestick holder and also moved in.

"You'll be leaving without a few things, or we'll be leaving you dead and you still lose your prize," Denton said and shrugged. "Your choice!"

"Yeah," said Theryn, his voice now full of confidence and determination.

Granny looked as if she were about to hand everything over but stopped suddenly, quickly tightening her arms around the items. She shrugged, looking for all the world as if she wasn't concerned. "Nope. If you want these, you have to come take them!" At the same time, she gave Mia a bit of a shove in the lower back.

"Oh, no," murmured Mia. She took a deep breath, momentarily closed her eyes, then she roared into battle. In very fast moves, she hastily blocked the pipe from hitting her head and kicked Theryn in the chest, causing him to lose his balance. Willard rushed Mia from behind, but was soon blocked by Max.

Working back to back, Max and Mia fended off every angry charge the two thugs made. Kicks flew, a fist to a thug's chest, the heel of a palm to a chin, a kick to a knee, a chop to a neck.

Morris wasn't sure what to do when Denton headed for him. "I owe you for putting me in that prison, Morris," he snarled. "Do you have any idea what that's like?"

"No, Denton, I don't, but I'm sure it won't be your last time there, so you better get used to it."

Denton smirked. Then his eyes narrowed.

"You know I'll be informing the authorities that you escaped, don't you? No, wait. I already have."

"Well, you see, that's the thing. No one realizes I'm gone, nor will they. So even if you made a call, the people at the prison are going to assure you that I'm in my cell."

Morris said, "What makes you think I called the prison. I put in a call to authorities here. I figure I'd let them pick you up and sort it out later."

Denton lunged. Morris dodged, and he took off at a dead run to the other side of the house. "I knew I should have gone to karate practice!" he panted under his breath. As he rounded the corner, Denton tackled him. "AAHHHH!" spewed from his mouth as he fell to the ground, his legs trapped in Denton's grip.

Morris struggled fiercely. Denton shifted position, sitting on his chest, his hands moving swiftly to his throat, trying to choke him, fury in his ice-blue eyes, pent-up anger finally unleashed.

Morris cast about for help, but everyone seemed to be occupied, at least everyone he could see from his position on the floor. He fought Denton, but the man had far more strength. Morris could feel the hands at his throat tightening. It was hard to breathe.

Out of desperation, Morris brought his knee up and jammed it into Denton's side. It was enough of a distraction for Denton to loosen his grip and rise slightly. Morris lifted both his legs and kicked Denton away from him as hard as he could. The man's body hit a bookcase, and a bust of Einstein tumbled off the top shelf and crashed onto Denton's head. The man crumpled. Morris scrambled up and bolted across the room. He ducked when a book came flying in his direction from somewhere. It hit the front window, shattering the lower pane. It was then Morris heard it, the wail of sirens. Was that the police? The others must have heard it too because the sound of fighting quickly became a scramble for escape. In a flash the two thugs broke off fighting. Theryn and Willard grabbed Denton by the arms and pulled him to a back window. By the time Denton groggily came to, they had the window open and shoved him through it.

But the Crypto-Capers were just as anxious to leave. With Dante not there, they had no intention of spending the next several hours or days trying to explain their presence in his house with it a total wreck. Max and Mia grapped Morris and exited the front door in a flash. The police were a few blocks away, but they'd be there in seconds. They jumped in the van. Without a word, Mr. Weedlesome drove off in the opposite direction of the approaching police.

ELEVEN

PANTING AND WITH HEARTS RACING, it was several minutes before anyone could speak.

"That was close," wheezed Max as he wiped the back of his hand over his sweaty brow.

"I know, but—" replied Mia. She had started to grin, but it fell instantly. "Where's Granny?"

Max said, "She made a run for it when the fight broke out. I'm not sure where she went."

"I hope she didn't get lost somewhere," commented Mr. Weedlesome, his hands gripped tightly on the steering wheel, his shoulders hunched and tense.

Morris said, "We'll find out soon enough. Dad, did you by any chance bring my laptop?"

"Oh, yeah. It's in the black case behind your seat. Why?"

Morris snatched the black case, hastily extracted the laptop, and opened it. He pressed a few buttons, tapping his fingers nervously on the thumbpad as it booted. The laptop was, of course, encrypted to prevent the wrong person from seeing something they shouldn't. Morris's fingers splayed across the buttons quickly as the screen popped up and showed a picture of the team as its background. After pressing a few more buttons and moving his fingertips across the mouse pad, a screen popped up with a map. A bright red dot moved across it. "We're live and running. Max, if you could please." Max pressed a button on his watch phone.

"Granny, can you hear me?"

"Yes, dear. Of course I can hear you." She sounded surprisingly calm and relaxed.

"Do you have on the new glasses I gave you?" asked Morris.

Granny's long pause gave her away. "No, Morris, I don't. To be honest, I thought they made me look old."

Morris glanced at his companions for some help, but they were too flabbergasted to retort. How do you respond to a comment like that? "Well, Granny, they were out of the star-and-moon-shaped glasses you wanted—all the kiddies bought them. Those are the most popular styles right now, you know." Morris's tone was filled with sarcasm.

"Don't be silly, dear, but they could at least have given them some pizzazz. These are just plain, black, rectangular glasses. Boring. I mean, *really*, where is the personality in that?"

Morris laughed and shook his head. "I bought what was available, and . . . and . . . well, there are times when you need to look professional."

"Professional? I've worked my whole life in this business. I have the respect of seven governments—"

"Granny, please, just put them on," encouraged Max.

"Oh, all right!"

Morris watched his screen. He had already activated the glasses and watched as they came out of the darkness of Granny's handbag. For just a second, he thought he saw red eyes blink at him. Then he got a view of damp floor and Granny's peach-colored orthotic shoes, illuminated by her flashlight. One of her socks had fallen and pooled at her ankle revealing a skinny, bony shin. Then the glasses came up, and, after a bit of wobbling, settled on Granny's nose.

"They better be the right prescription," she was saying rather put out, "that's all I have to say."

"They are. I'm not an idiot." Then Morris concentrated on the computer screen that was seeing everything Granny was seeing. She was in a rounded tunnel surrounded by rock.

"Where are you?" asked Mia, peering at the screen over Morris's shoulder.

"I'm in an underground tunnel beneath the city. Where it leads, I have no idea. I discovered it behind the fireplace in the spare bedroom."

Emmanuel, sitting in the front seat, turned suddenly. "I know where that tunnel leads. I've taken it dozens of times. Grandfather is sometimes hesitant to go out in public. For obvious reasons. He uses that tunnel to get where he needs to go undetected. It's actually kinda cool. Granny, you'll come to several forks in the tunnel, but each time one way seems to veer off and one continues straight. You need to keep going straight until you reach a set of stairs and a ramp. That'll lead you to the back of a library in a quiet section of the city where only people with keys can enter." Emmanuel sat back a moment and dug for something in his pocket. "And, yes! It just so happens, I have one of those keys with me." The key was gold, small, with a rounded, slightly indented top.

"Your grandfather . . . has his own section in the library?" asked Max, looking at the key.

Emmanuel shrugged. "Sure. It's simple really. He's one of the benefactors. He donated thousands of dollars to the library, gave them rare books. There was a time when it needed renovations, and the university couldn't afford it. Grandfather stepped in and gave them the money."

"University?" asked Mia.

"Yes, the library is at the University of Pisa. If we could start heading there now, Mr. Weedlesome. Do you know where it is?"

Mr. Weedlesome nodded. "I've worked for them."

Max thought for several minutes. "I'm sure there were certain terms to the arrangement Dante made, terms that include the secret room." Max smiled as conclusions fell into place. "Dante was brilliant," said Max and he motioned for Emmanuel to put the key back into his pocket. "Where could he go from there? I mean, these tunnels have to lead to his secret hide-out."

Emmanuel sighed. "He's never told me that."

"Then we really don't know where to go yet."

"Sure, we do, Max," began Morris. "We turned up several things in the house—a note card with a name on it, a journal, and a map . . . as well as the cryptex."

Max frowned. "Yes, but we never had a chance to look at any of them, and Granny has all those things with her. Doesn't she?"

"Not exactly!" Morris reached into his back pocket and pulled out a piece of paper "I removed this from the cryptex. I wasn't sure what Granny was going to do, so I opened it and removed what was inside."

Mia reached for the paper, and Morris gave it to her. She carefully unfolded it. Inside was a cryptogram.

G I T F S C	P M	K O S F B A C G

Mia immediately got out her pencil.

"What does it say?" asked Morris.

"Give me a minute to figure it out." Mia got out her note pad and flipped to the cipher key she had used to solve the other cryptogram earlier. She instantly began to decode the message. Then she spoke the answer aloud.

"What is that?" blurted Mr. Weedlesome from the front seat.

Emmanuel said, "In Italy, it can only be one place. The Piazza dei Miracoli. The name was created by the Italian writer and poet Gabriele d' Annunzio. It contains several buildings of importance. The Tower of Pisa is there, along with the Duomo, the Bapistry, and the Camposanto."

"Those are religious edifices, correct?" said Max.

"Yes! The square is known as the Piazzo del Duomo, which means, 'Cathedral Square.' It's a wide, walled area at the heart of the city of Pisa. It's recognized as one of the main centers for medieval art in the world."

"Really?" said Mia, and she smiled. "I love art."

"Then you'll love what's inside some of those amazing buildings."

"Ah-hem! I'd like to get out of here," spouted Granny impatiently through the watch phone.

"Sorry. Keep walking straight," said Emmanuel.

The group watched the computer screen as Granny walked down the tunnel. After some time she stopped in a large, spacious room with high ceilings. It, too, was constructed of rock. As she looked ahead of her she noticed a stone bridge and on the other side was a circular staircase rising up through the ceiling above.

Emmanuel squinted and frowned at the laptop screen. "I don't recognize that bridge or those stairs. Did you turn somewhere?"

"When was the last time you came down here, Emmanuel?" asked Granny. "There were literally a dozen turns and corridors before I got to this spot. I have no idea where I'm going." By Granny's tone the group could tell that she was on edge.

"Calm down, Granny, we'll figure this out," said Max as he looked at his companions.

Morris said, "Walk closer to the bridge, Granny. Let me get a better look at it."

As Granny walked closer, Morris seemed to move closer to the screen, his mouth dropping open.

"Oh, my gosh, what's that?"

The bridge formed a very narrow path. There were no railings. The walkway across was only a few inches thick and made of differently sized blocks set on two beams. The blocks were big enough for someone to step on, and carved on their tops were Mayan numbers.

"Is that what I think it is?" Max asked.

"If you think you're seeing Mayan numbers, you're correct," said Morris. "We're definitely in the right place. That bridge is a test, too. I'm sure of it."

"How many blocks would you say are on that bridge?" Max asked.

Granny counted them. "Thirty blocks in all, but some are pretty small. I figure I only need to step on maybe ten to get across."

"Yes, but that's the trick, isn't it? Which ten blocks?" said Mia.

"Maybe you can just turn around and go a different way," offered Mr. Weedlesome from the driver's seat.

Granny heard the suggestion, and immediately followed the advice. She turned on her heels to retrace her steps down the tunnel, but before she could exit the large room, a solid stone wall lowered in front of her, blocking the way. Dust from the rock scraping against the surrounding rock clouded up. Granny began to cough, and she covered her mouth and nose with her hand, then a scarf she pulled from her bag. When the cloud of dust dissipated, Granny—and those watching in the van—saw no way out. In frustration, she pressed her forehead and hands on the block.

"Why does this always happen to me?" she grumbled, the words muffled by the scarf. After taking a deep breath, Granny pushed away from the rock, pulled down the scarf and walked resolutely back towards the bridge. "That's the only way out now. You guys better think of something. That's all I have to say."

"We're working on it," replied Morris. As Granny waited, she looked around the room, and everyone watched the screen, looking for something that might help. The walls appeared solid. The bridge crossed empty space black with shadow. As Granny got the nerve to peer over the side and shone her flashlight down, everyone saw water about ten feet below the bridge. Not so bad, but the flashlight also revealed pointed rocks just under the surface that looked particularly sharp and jagged. Then Granny's flashlight illuminated part of a skeleton with a lance of rock coming up through its rib cage. If Granny fell, if the bridge had a pattern that must be followed and she misstepped, she would surely die a horrible death.

Granny raised her hand to her lips. "Oh, dear God." She backed up carefully, then plopped down on the ground, holding the items she had found in Dante's house in her lap.

"I was thinking," began Morris. He was running his hand through his hair in frustration, staring at the computer intently. "Look through the journal. Maybe we can find something in there that'll help."

Granny opened the journal and stared at the very first page. She perused the contents quickly, yet slowly enough for the others to see the details of the flashlight lit pages through her glasses.

"Morris, the information in here is immense, as well as valuable. Do you know that there are several undiscovered treasures lurking . . ."

"Oh, I saw that, Granny. Fodder for future adventures surely, but first let's focus on getting you out of there. Turn back a few pages. I think I saw something."

Granny did as she was told. "Tell me what you see." Granny turned the pages slowly.

"The writing is different. Marcello didn't write some of this."

"No, but I bet you money that Dante did. What else?"

"There's a cryptogram with circles on it, probably signifying that certain letters are important. You might want to let Mia take a better look at it." Morris pressed a few buttons on his keyboard, causing the view to zoom in. He then took a picture, blowing it up, and, inserted a piece of paper into the back of the laptop from his bag and actually printed out the picture. The paper disappeared into the laptop and returned out the same slot with the cryptogram printed on it.

"Here Mia, take a look," Morris handed the page over to her. She started working right away, her pencil moving furiously on the paper. It took her several minutes to accomplish the task, but in the end she had the results. Mia paused and stared off into space.

Max said, "What does it say already?"

Y P   H P T   X (U) P Z   D V F D   (O) D   O G

J C S H   J C S H   U C (B) C G G F S H   (M) P S

V P U C G D   Q C P Q A C   D P   S C K F (O) U

O U   F S D ?   V F S Y A H   F U H P U C

X U (P) Z G   D V F D   D V C   G C B S C D

P M   (E) C F T D O M T A   Z P S X   A O C G

D P   (F) N S C F D   C R D C U D   O U

D S T D V   F U Y   G O U (B) C S C

G C U D O K C U D .

Mia told them, then said, "Why would he have that in there? It makes no sense."

Emmanuel said, "Sure it does, but only to the right person. You know who said that, don't you?"

Only Mia seemed to have an inkling.

"Yes, Mia?"

"Vincent van Gogh said it. But why's that important?"

"My grandfather loved art. He said that artwork of any kind held a clear and unspoken truth. Van Gogh was one of his favorite painters. He keeps a replica of *Starry Night over the Rhone* and *The Starry Night* in his house. You probably saw them, but then again, with his house being dark, you maybe didn't."

"What do the circled letters mean?" interrupted Max.

Mia wrote down the answers from the circled letters from the cryptogram.

_____ _____ _____ _____ _____

_____ _____ _____ _____

Then she began to rearrange them, making various word combinations. It didn't take her long to figure out what they were supposed to say.

"_____

_____!"

"Obviously, the man's dead. So where's he buried?" Max's question was a good one, but one that had to wait.

Morris said, "First we have other questions to answer. For example, there are Mayan numbers on the cobblestone blocks, not letters. So what use is this information?"

"It can't be just thrown out there for fun," offered Max. "It has to mean *something*. Wait a minute!" Max raised his hand to his chin. "Each letter in the name means something. Out of curiosity, Mia, can you write down the alphabet for me?" Mia did as she was told.

"Now, each letter in the alphabet has a specific position. For example, A is the *first* letter of the alphabet, B is the *second*, C the *third*, and so on. Write down the number that each letter represents, if you please."

Mia began to write down the numbers on her notepad below the letters.

"All right," she said. "Now what?"

"Now take letters from our message and write down their numbers. After that, change those numbers into Mayan numbers. Do you remember how?"

"Sure!" Mia began to draw the shapes on her note pad. "The number one is represented by a circle like this. And the number five is represented by a rectangle that looks like this. I remember."

"Very good," said Max as he watched Mia draw the shapes with the letters.

"Watch me. Make sure I'm doing this right. The first letter is "F" and it's the sixth letter of the alphabet. So six would be represented the following way, correct?"

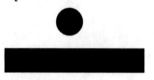

"Exactly, Mia. Please continue with the rest."

Mia began to fill in the rest of the Mayan numbers for the remaining letters. When Mia was finished, she held up the piece of paper for Morris to glance at.

"That looks good, Mia. Hey, Granny? I need you to move towards the bridge, please."

Granny rose from the ground and stepped close enough to the bridge for Morris to see the first few blocks of the bridge through her glasses. "Okay, I see the Mayan number for six on your right. Do you trust me?"

Without saying a word, Granny took a deep breath, glanced at the Mayan number, then stepped on it. Amazingly enough, the stone was solid. Granny exhaled sharply. "What are the next Mayan numbers?"

Mia told her the next number, then the next. One by one, step by step, Granny moved to the right and left of the bridge, stepping on the corresponding Mayan numbers until she made it to the last one. That block was of an awkward shape so when Granny stepped on it, her heel touched the neighboring block on the right side. When she did, that block disintegrated almost immediately leaving a gaping hole and a view of a place she did not want to end up. Granny quickly swung her body forward and stepped onto solid ground.

TWELVE

ONCE GRANNY REACHED THE OTHER SIDE, she carefully approached the spiral staircase. It was impressively crafted. The treads were slabs of stone stacked at one end to form a column and fanned out around that column in a spiral. There were no railings, and Granny eyed it suspiciously. She stepped up on the first tread hesitantly.

"If you're worried about traps—don't be," said Morris. "I was able to do a quick scan for them through your glasses and found nothing. The bridge was the test."

Granny's pace up the stairs began to quicken. With each step, Granny felt more and more apprehensive. With each step, should the stairway give way, she was further and further from the floor. More than that, she had no idea what she'd find above her. As she came to the top of the staircase, she noticed a wood door to her left. It had no key hole so Granny assumed that it was not locked. Granny raised her hand slowly and placed it on the doorknob. It was cold and moved only with difficulty as she turned it. Then she pushed.

The door was heavy and loud as it squeaked open, leading Granny into a small room with bookshelves almost covering every wall. There was a small table and a couple of chairs, as well as a roll-top desk to her left. A painting filled the open space on one wall, and it seemed familiar to Granny, but she couldn't place it. "Now what?" she asked as she scanned the room.

Emmanuel pointed at the computer screen. "You're in my grandfather's secret room at the library." He glanced at his watch. "Ten-thirty. I didn't realize it was so late. The library closes at eleven. The room is on the main floor towards the back of the building. The library itself is towards the center of campus. It does have some security, but we should have no problem getting in and out quickly. Granny, since you don't have the key to get yourself out of the room, you'll have to wait for us to come open the door from the other side." Emmanuel raised his head and focused on the driver's seat. "Are we almost there, Mr. Weedlesome?"

"Few more minutes."

Being always economical in effort, Granny sat at the table in the middle of the room and propped her feet up on the second chair. "I'll be here," she said as she placed her hands on her stomach and leaned back.

She was facing the painting. The more she stared at it the more she was convinced she was looking at a work by Vincent van Gogh. The problem was, the strokes were inconsistent and raw, almost inexperienced. The painting didn't have the enthusiasm and intensity of van Gogh either. As she stared at it, she began to believe it actually might look better if turned upside down.

Granny got up and went to the painting. She lifted it down, rotated it and put it back up. Indeed, the picture looked considerably better. Now it was a scene of the Tower of Pisa and in front of it stood three people. The two men and a woman were almost connected at the hips as they held in their hands a Golden Monkey. The statue was very detailed though the faces of the three people were distorted, impressionistic. Granny had a good idea who the three were and as she looked at the signature of the artist in the lower right hand corner—sure enough, Dante's name was there, not Van Gogh's.

Granny returned to her chair and sat again, but this time she took her camera from her bag and took several pictures of the painting, including a close-up of the monkey statue. When she lowered the camera, she again studied the painting. She noticed a kind of arrow in the brush-strokes of the background paint pointing to the left side of the room. As Granny followed the wall, she spied the roll top desk. Knowing how creative and mysterious Dante was, Granny headed to the desk. Layers of dust indicated it had not been touched in some time. Granny sneezed as she raised the cover, and the dust was disturbed.

On top of the desk was only one thing, a unique black, rectangular box held shut with a silver clasp. Granny picked up the box and checked its weight. She then rotated the box until she'd studied it from every angle. The box was made of black leather, its corners covered in decorative silver. The clasp was unique in nature as it required someone to rotate a dial to the right or left to open it. Thinking that the box was important, Granny kept it when she closed the cover on the desk and sat back down, setting the box on the table in front of her. Always the curious one, Granny used one finger to rotate the dial to the right one time, but the clasp didn't release. She then rotated it twice to the left, but it still held firm. After breathing in deeply and exhaling a long breath, Granny returned the dial back to its original spot, hoping to clear out her attempt.

She glanced at the painting, looking for guidance. The arrow to the left could have been a clue to something else, and the three people in the picture might have something to do with the solution. So Granny turned the dial to the left and rotated it three times. When she did, the clasp sprang open. A smile spread over Granny's lips as she carefully raised the lid of the box, her face angled away just in case. What she found inside, resting on a velvet cushion, was a thin piece of gold metal the length and shape of a bookmark.

The strip of gold was like nothing Granny had ever seen before, nor anything she might have expected. She figured it must be very old. Being gold, however, it looked absolutely clean and bright, giving no real clue its age other than the old, decorative style and the wear to the edges of some details.

Granny carefully lifted the object. The coolness of it almost caused her to shiver. It was heavy, telling her it was pure gold. She then carefully turned it over, analyzing every detail. It was a key, she decided. The end of the key was in the shape of a sun and looked similar to a picture she had seen at Chichen Itza. In fact, it looked very much like the sun on the sundial they already possessed.

Granny shifted it to her other hand to study the handle. It was unique. There was an oval, and both sides had Mayan numbers imprinted on them. On one side was the number three and, on the other, the number two.

"Are you seeing this, Morris?"

"I can see it, Granny," replied Mia. "I'm here in the van while the boys went inside to find you. I think you found something very important there. The markings are very similar to the sundial. I must say I was impressed with how you figured out how to open the box. I wrote down the Mayan numbers on the handle and drew a quick sketch of the whole key—it is a key, isn't it?"

"Oh, I'm pretty sure of that much," said Granny. "Its definitely Mayan, and probably opens something. What, though, I have no idea."

Granny was about to return the key to its home in the box, when she saw a piece of paper sticking up from one edge of the velvet. It was the same color as the velvet, so Granny almost missed it. Granny carefully lifted the velvet panel, then took up the paper. On it was a cryptogram.

"Mia!" she shouted.

"I see it, Granny. Give me a minute, I'm writing it down." After several seconds past, Mia continued with, "Got it!"

Granny placed the cryptogram and the key back into the box and closed the lid. She then rotated the dial three times to clear it. The lock clicked into place. After

D P   P Q C U,   D V C   D S C F G T S C

S P P K ,   D V C   X C H   O G   D V C

F U G Z C S .

perusing the outside of the box a few more times, Granny put the box and the other items they had found-carefully inside her handbag. She then turned to the door as a sound had just come from there.

Granny instantly became alert. She rose, pulling the box back out of her bag in the same motion. Then she stooped and slid it under the roll-top desk. With it safe, she brought back her handbag as if handling a bat, ready to strike an intruder. She approached the door.

The lock clicked and the knob turned, and Granny readied herself for mortal defense. The door swung open, revealing Morris, Max, and Emmanuel. Granny exhaled a deep breath of relief and lowered her handbag. "It's about time, boys. I was starting to worry."

Granny retrieved the box and put it back in her bag. As everyone left, Emmanuel gave the room a quick glance before closing and locking the door behind them. He then followed behind as Max led them back down the hallway and out of the library. Mr. Weedlesome had parked the van at the curb at the bottom of the stairs. It was running, ready to take off as soon as they got in.

When the foursome descended the stairs, Mia opened the door and slid over. Granny climbed into the front passenger seat, and Emmanuel, Morris, and Max piled in with Mia in the back seats. Once everyone was situated, Mr. Weedlesome took off.

"Are you all right, Nellie?" asked Mr. Weedlesome as he glanced over her.

"I'm fine, thank you." Granny raised her hand and yawned loudly. Her appearance was certainly haggard. Her clothes were covered in dirt and cobwebs. Her usually neat hair was coming out of its bun and long strands hung by her face making her look like a wild woman.

"I think we've all had a long day. I say we call it a night," suggested Max.

"I agree," said Morris.

Mr. Weedlesome said, "My hotel's nearby. Let me make a phone call." Mr. Weedlesome took out his cell phone and made a call. Within minutes he closed the phone and smiled. "I reserved the connecting room to mine. Emmanuel and Morris can stay with me while you, Mia, and Max can take the other room."

Granny glanced over at Mr. Weedlesome and smiled weakly. "Thanks, dear. We appreciate everything you've done to help us."

"No problem. For the first time, it's exciting to be a part of one of my son's adventures." Mr. Weedlesome glanced towards the back seat at Morris, who was beginning to nod off, before continuing his drive to the hotel.

THIRTEEN

THE TEAM SLEPT IN the next morning, not waking until almost noon. All the excitement over the past few days had worn them out.

With the sun bright in the autumn sky, Max rose, his body and mind rested. He could now think about yesterday's events. So many things had happened, and yet they seemed no closer to their goal than a week ago. The more Max thought about it, though, the more he knew that wasn't true. They had made progress in the past day. Maybe it was the feeling that they were being preyed upon by the Panther's accomplices, as well as the Panther's own son. Or, maybe it was the fact that they still had so far to go. It seemed like they had the right idea about what was going on, he thought, and the objects they found surely would help them, and yet it was the lack of confirmation that made Max feel uneasy about it all. They needed time to analyze what they had.

Wanting some fresh air to clear his troubled mind, Max made his way over to the balcony to see the streets below. They were staying at the Hotel Bologna right in the heart of Pisa, one of the most prestigious hotels in the city. He thought Mr. Weedlesome's work afforded a few luxuries at least.

Max glanced back at the hotel room, which he had paid no attention to the night before. It was magnificent. The décor seemed fresh and clean with ochre, peach and green tones. The room was spacious, luxurious and comfortable. It definitely had an air of elegance about it. Max returned his attention to the streets below. He was thinking about how they were going to find Liliana Staletti, when he saw a woman on a scooter drive on the street below with an advertising sign on the side. Max read the words and almost stopped breathing. The sign was for a tour guide, and in big bold letters was the name—Liliana Staletti.

Max bolted from the room, not bothering to tell anyone where he was going and ran down the hallway towards the stairwell. Before the door was a window. A quick glance told him the scooter was waiting at a light in traffic in front of the hotel. Max pushed through the door and skipped down the stairs. Their room was only on the second floor, so he didn't have too far to go. Max pushed through the door at the bottom of the stairwell and sprinted to the front sliding doors. Liliana was just beginning to pass him when he arrived at the street. Max began to shout and wave his arms to get her attention. She was just stepping on the gas, when she saw him waving, then pointing towards the sign on her scooter. She pulled over to the curb.

Max had been running so hard that he raised his arms above his head to catch his breath.

Liliana took off her helmet and stared at him as if he were crazy. Max returned the stare, analyzing Liliana's every feature. She was dressed completely in light blue, from the barrettes in her silver-blonde hair to her moccasin-covered feet. Lying loosely around her neck hung a silver chain with a small charm at the end. Her jeans were stylish and flared at the bottom. As Max studied her face, her genuine beauty charmed him. Her hair was perfectly straight and looked as smooth and soft as silk. Her eyes were large and sky blue. Her skin was slightly tan and clear of all imperfections. The sparkle in her eyes showed her lust for life.

"Are you Liliana Staletti?" he finally managed to get out.

"Yes. What can I help you with?" asked Liliana, her tone a bit sharp.

"Several things, actually, but first, introductions. I'm Max, Maxwell Holmes, and I'm a detective. I'm here on a case."

Liliana was just in the process of smiling when Max pulled out his detective badge and showed it to her She blinked. "How can I assist you . . . detective?"

"Please, call me Max. And, if you wouldn't mind following me into the hotel out of earshot from strangers, I'll tell you exactly how you can help me."

Liliana's eyes narrowed.

"You can trust me, Liliana."

"And who am I going to find inside, Maxwell?"

"The rest of my team."

Liliana thought for several seconds.

"No, I don't think so. Good day." Liliana put on her helmet and revved the engine.

Max blurted, "Do you know a Dante de Luca?"

Liliana's gaze snapped to Max, her features turning serious.

"Come with me if you care about him at all! I'm here because of him."

Liliana took several deep breaths, not moving for some time. Then she turned off her scooter and stepped away.

"Fine. Let's go," Liliana said, clearly not liking her decision.

A hotel doorman came out and began yelling something in Italian. Liliana explained why her scooter was parked where it was and asked the man to watch it for her. The man was disgruntled, but agreed. Max reached into his wallet and pulled out some cash to sweeten the arrangement. The man shoved the money into his pocket and smiled, bowing slightly while taking Liliana's helmet. Max led the way into the hotel, this time opting for the elevator, which he hoped she'd find more acceptable than the stairs. Liliana followed quietly.

Back in the room the group was up and already going over the items they had found. On the table was the journal, the guide book, and information about the Camposanto Monumentale. Granny also had laid out the black leather box she'd found in the library. She was talking about it with the rest of the group when Max walked in.

The connecting door was open between the rooms and Morris, Emmanuel, and Mr. Weedlesome were all standing at that door while Granny and Mia sat at the table just inside the door. As soon as Max came in, Granny popped up from her chair ready to pounce on him for running out of the room the way he had without telling anyone where he was going, but she stopped when she saw the pretty face of Liliana behind him.

"Where did you go, Max? You had me worried?" Granny glanced from Max to Liliana, waiting.

"Team," said Max with a smile, "we had a stroke of luck. This is Liliana Staletti, our new tour guide."

All eyes were now on Liliana. She glanced at each person in turn, clearly not recognizing any of them, until her gaze fell on Emmanuel. A connection between them was clear. They knew each other.

"Lily? Is that you?" Emmanuel stepped closer, clearly surprised.

Liliana's thin lips broke into a smile, revealing even white teeth. "Emmanuel?" Liliana ran to him and hugged him. "I can't believe it's you. You've grown. What are you doing here, cousin?"

"I'm helping the Crypto-Capers solve a case."

Mia said, "You and Emmanuel are cousins?"

"Yes, our mothers are sisters." Liliana stepped away from Emmanuel and glared at him. "This is about Grandfather isn't it?"

"You know it is. What are you doing in Pisa, Lily? The last I heard you were in Spain with your parents."

"And they're still there. I chose to come and help Grandfather alone. He needs it."

"Liliana, you have to tell us where he's going. We need him to know. People are after him."

Liliana turned away from Emmanuel. "I don't know where he went. All I know is that he's gone. He said people were after him, but he also said that people were trying to help him. I don't know what to believe." Liliana paused for several seconds, taking deep breaths to calm herself. "He mentioned the name Morris, a Morris Weedlesome? Is there a Morris here?"

Morris stepped forward, his hand raised halfway. Liliana rushed towards him, grasping his hands in hers. Morris' cheeks became slightly flushed as he stared into Liliana's blue eyes. "Grandfather said that you were going to redeem him. Is this true?"

"I . . . I . . . I don't know about *redeeming* him, but we're trying to *help* him, yes."

"He believes in you, Morris, and if my grandfather believes in a person, then that person must have showed him loyalty. I'll help you if I can. Show me what you've found."

Liliana held onto one of Morris's hands tightly. Morris wasn't sure what to do except follow along beside her as she made her way to the table where Granny had the items of their adventure displayed.

"All right, well, first, this guide book and information is for the Camposanto Monumentale, which is a monumental cemetery."

"Yes, we're focusing on this. Can you tell us what you know about it?" asked Granny.

"Sure! It lies in the northern edge of the cathedral square. It's a walled cemetery, which some have claimed to be the most beautiful in the world. I take tourists there all the time. It's an amazing place. It's said to have been built around five shiploads of sacred soil from Golgotha. If you're Roman Catholic, you'll know that Golgotha is where Christ was crucified. The soil was brought back to Pisa from the fourth crusade by an archbishop. Inside is a huge collection of Roman sculptures and sarcophagi. The years and wars have done their damage, though, and now there are only around eighty-four sarcophagi left. Many frescoes decorate the walls and the ceilings. They are amazing to behold. The intricacies and the detail are simply wonderful.

"Majority of the frescoes have been removed for conservation reasons and are now displayed in a gallery. They were severely damaged in the Second World War, when the roof fell in during Allied bombardment. Many frescoes were ruined by the elements. If you get a chance to see these frescoes, please do. A few of the damaged ones can still be seen in the Camposanto, the most fascinating of which is the fourteenth-century *Triumph of Death*. A room off one side of the cloister displays historical photos of the frescoes before and after the bombing in 1944. The cemetery was the burial place for Pisa's upper class.

"Now, in the cathedral square are other buildings that I don't see information on. You have the Duomo, which is a medieval cathedral. You also have the Leaning

Tower, which is also known as the cathedral's campanile. Then there is the Baptistry and the Camposanto. You have four great religious edifices in that one place and they hold a lot of history."

"Why would Grandfather have information on the Camposanto?" asked Emmanuel.

"Probably because of Grandmother and Marcello. We have relatives buried there from long ago. They adored the place and family visited it often."

"I know, but . . ." stammered Emmanuel.

Max stepped forward to help him. "You said there are sculptures inside. Is there one of Pisa's own Fibonacci?"

Liliana stared at Max with a look of confusion. "Leonardo Fibonacci? Of course! In the nineteenth century, a statue of him was erected in Pisa. It's located in the western gallery of the Camposanto against a wall. It's been moved several times over the years for different reasons, but it's been restored and been in the Camposanto since 1990. Many people feel that's where it belongs. I've seen it many times, and Grandfather visits it often. It's beautiful."

"Really?" chimed in Morris, trying to get free of Liliana's grasp without it seeming to be an issue, but she wasn't letting go.

"Yes!" Morris stopped his struggling, a thought coming to him. "I know where he's hidden the other pieces. In the statue of Fibonacci. He must have. That's why he used Fibonacci numbers, and why we're here in Pisa now. It all boils down to Leonardo."

The team had known that Fibonacci was a part of it all, but they didn't know how. Morris made sense. They knew they needed to check out the statue in that cemetery.

Max said, "Given the fact that the statue's been moved around quite a bit over the years, Dante's had time to hide the pieces safely, creating opportunity for himself by using what was available to him at the time. Morris, old buddy, I believe you figured it out."

Liliana pointed towards the box. "What's that? I haven't seen anything like that before."

"I have!" said Emmanuel, and everyone looked at him. "It's a key. What it opens though, I don't know. I've seen Grandfather open that case once or twice. When I opened it up once out of curiosity, he was angry. It was then he hid it. When I had asked him about it and why he didn't want me to see it. He said it wasn't my time. This was a few years ago, but I don't know what that means."

"It means you weren't ready for the responsibility of what this key opens," said Granny. "But I feel you are now. There was a message in the box, hidden under the bottom piece of velvet. It is a cryptogram. I was just about to verify with Mia what she had wrote down in her notepad earlier." Granny handed Mia the paper.

Liliana glanced at her watch as she listened to Granny. "I need to go. I'm late." She turned to Morris and squeezed his hand, smiling sweetly. "Walk me out?"

Morris glanced at Mia and Granny, who smiled and encouraged him, then back at Liliana, not quite sure what to say. "Uh . . . oh, sure, I can do that."

Liliana turned towards her cousin. "*Tutto sarà tutto il di destra. Ho un programma. Arrivederci.*" She then turned to the rest of the group. "I'm sure I'll be seeing all of you again. It's been a pleasure."

Liliana then led the way out, not once letting go of Morris's hand. Morris, looking very red about the ears, closed the hotel room door behind them as they headed to the stairs. The short jaunt down the staircase and into the lobby was quiet and uneventful. When they were outdoors at last, Liliana thanked the doorman as he handed her the helmet and walked back into the hotel. Liliana took a step closer to Morris.

"My grandfather says you're a whiz when it comes to computers, that you work for a computer company fixing them. You fixed his as well as a few other things around his house. Is that true? And this isn't the time to be cavalier."

"My dad works for a computer company. I just help him on occasion. And, yes, I did fix Dante's computer and stuff. I'm also the computer geek for my team, so to say that I know something about computers would certainly be true."

Liliana narrowed her eyes. "Grandfather knows you'll succeed on your quest. His faith in you is unyielding, but there's something still in shadow."

"In shadow?" questioned Morris, not quite sure what Liliana was talking about.

"In doubt. You'll open the treasure room. We all know this, but, in the end, who will get the treasure? You?

Or the enemy? If it came to that, it certainly would be a shame." Liliana took several deep breaths. "I feel that the enemy can still win even after you've done everything in your power to prevent it from happening."

Morris wasn't sure what she was leading up to. Slowly, Liliana reached into her back pocket and pulled out a piece of paper, tucking it into Morris's palm. Morris carefully unfolded the paper and stared at it. What he saw was a series of numbers, almost like dimensions. There was also a drawing and . . . a weight.

"What does Dante want me to do?"

"He wants you to think about it," replied Liliana sweetly. Morris had an idea of what Dante wanted him to do, but wasn't quite sure how to pull it off.

"Noted. I'll consider it."

"That's all any of us can ask," responded Liliana, as her eyes searched the depths of Morris's.

"Do you always carry this information with you everywhere you go?"

Liliana smiled. "No, not usually. Do you think I drove past here by accident on my way to work?"

Morris smiled and shook his head. "There are no accidents!"

"No," Liliana agreed, "there aren't. I was looking for you . . . have been for some time. It was fate that Max found me when he did."

Morris shook his head, having a hard time believing Liliana. She was clever, but deceiving. "I'll need your cell phone number," she said, "so I can get hold of you."

Morris told Liliana the number. She programmed it into her cell phone, then put the phone back into her pocket. "It'd be senseless for you and your team to visit the cemetery during the day to analyze the statue. There are too many tourists, and you'll be seen. The best time would be at night when no one's around. The museum closes at four-thirty. It gets dark early this time of year. At around seven o'clock, there'll be a . . . hiccup in the security system, and the head guard will need someone to come and fix it right away." Liliana handed Morris a map and began pointing to it as she spoke.

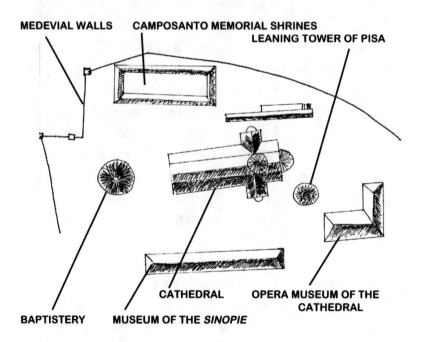

MEDEVIAL WALLS   **CAMPOSANTO MEMORIAL SHRINES**

LEANING TOWER OF PISA

CATHEDRAL   **OPERA MUSEUM OF THE CATHEDRAL**

BAPTISTERY   **MUSEUM OF THE *SINOPIE***

"You'll enter to the right side of the field by the Opera Museum. No vehicles are allowed near any of the sites. Tourists usually get dropped off by bus near the closest gate, which is to the left side of the Baptistery known as the Porta di Santa Maria, and walk in from there. The elongated building next to the cemetery is where security is. The system is located towards the center of that building. You'll be able to park outside that building only and walk in from there.

"The security system runs throughout each site in the Campo dei Miracoli. As you can imagine, there's a lot of history and valuable items here. Let's see, there are several cameras in the Baptistery, the Cathedral, the Leaning Tower, the Opera Museum, the Museum of the Sinopie, along the medevial walls of course, which surround the majority of the Campo dei Miracoli, and then the Camposanto Monumentale, or the cemetery. I'd give you the current information about the security company they're using, but I believe you already know that. It was installed by your father's company." Liliana paused, then continued. "I'll come by and offer my assistance in trying to solve problems, coming up with some excuse as to why I'm there. Make sure you or your father receives the call."

Morris knew exactly what Liliana was implying and nodded in understanding.

"You won't be able to bring the whole team, so I suggest bringing Max with you. I'll help you under the condition that Emmanuel stays well out of harm's way. If he's caught, you won't be able to continue with your quest."

"Why? What's so special about Emmanuel that you and your grandfather are both willing to spare him?"

"All I can say is that he's the key to all this. You made a promise to my grandfather, and now you need to keep it. My grandfather trusts you, Morris, and so do I. This will be your only chance to take a look at that statue and find whatever you think is there. Take it running and ask no questions. We'll talk more later. *Arrivederci!*"

Liliana leaned forward and kissed Morris on the cheek before putting her helmet on. Without even a second glance, she sped off into traffic.

FOURTEEN

"LILIANA IS YOUR COUSIN?" asked Mia. She had waited until after Morris and Liliana had left the room to ask it.

"Yes," replied Emmanuel curtly, staring at the closed door.

"She's very—interesting."

"My cousin is definitely that, but she's also just showed us where her loyalties are," retorted Emmanuel.

"I thought they were with you. You're kin, after all."

"I'm family, but she has a new ally now," answered Emmanuel.

"Who? Morris?" spouted Mia.

"Didn't you not notice Liliana's behavior?" began Max as he stared at his sister in amazement. "As soon as she knew Morris was here, she grabbed his hand and held on tight. She showed us that she trusts him and him alone."

"How can she make that judgment so quickly? She knows nothing about us to make such a call," said Mia, frustrated and a little confused. "Do you think Morris met her before and just didn't mention it?"

"No," inserted Mr. Weedlesome firmly. "When Morris feels comfortable around a girl, he talks smoothly and has a touch of arrogance in his tone. But when he's uncomfortable—like with that girl—he stutters and has a hard time gathering his thoughts. I'd say he's never met Liliana before."

"Then it can only mean one thing. She had prior knowledge about us and knew who she could trust." deduced Max.

"More to the point," said Emmanuel, "it means she spoke with my grandfather—and recently."

"Precisely! She made her alliances before even walking into the room," replied Max.

"She knows something then," said Mia.

Granny nodded. "But will she share?"

At that moment, Morris walked back into the room. He seemed somewhat in a daze.

"Are you all right, son?" asked Mr. Weedlesome.

"Yes, Dad, I'm fine. We won't be able to go to the cemetery until tonight. Too many tourists. Liliana has a plan to get us in. Dad, she's going to disrupt the security system . . . somehow . . . that your company put in."

"That's right, we do run that system. I totally forgot about it. I should have come up with the idea myself," Mr. Weedlesome said.

"It's fine, Dad. She's going to make sure the guards call you to fix the problem. She'll mention that you're in the area. You need to make sure to take the call to get us in."

"No problem, Morris. I can also look up the information about the security system and see what they have. I wasn't the one who originally installed it, though. Another tech at the company did."

"What do you need us to do?" asked Granny.

"Max'll need to come with me tonight," Morris said. "Mia and Dad can be in the van in case we need them. But, Granny, I need you and Emmanuel to stay here and look through Dante's journal to make sure we aren't missing anything. The smallest detail might crush us."

"I want to go with you," said Emmanuel. "I know I can be of help."

"Yeah . . . no! I know you could help, but because of the dire situation and the fact that people are after your grandfather, we can't risk you being taken. You'd be leverage. You know too much, and they'd punish you or your grandfather for it. No, we need you to stay here where you're safe. I know that doesn't sound like fun, but believe me it won't be fun if you're caught."

Emmanuel, looking disgruntled and disappointed, nodded in understanding.

"We need to prep for later. Granny, begin to check on plane tickets for our return trip to Chichen Itza. I'll make contact with Pablo, see what's going on there. I have a feeling that, if we find tonight what I think we'll find, we'll need to get out of here as quickly as possible. Denton and his thugs are surely lurking around somewhere. We can't let them get their hands on anything of importance. The sooner we leave, the soon-

er we can solve this mystery." Morris paused before saying, "You all know what to do. If you'll excuse me for a
minute, I need to take care of something on my end."
Morris walked over to his laptop, picked it up and took
it into the other room. The group could hear him typing
furiously. The rest of the team broke up, focusing their
attentions on the preparations for the evening.

FIFTEEN

BY NIGHTFALL, MR. WEEDLESOME received the call from security that the system needed attention. Morris, Mr. Weedlesome, Max, and Mia left immediately. It didn't take long for them to reach the parking lot of the building next to the cemetery. Once they arrived, Max and Morris stepped out of the van. Mr. Weedlesome had loaned Max a company uniform to wear. Morris grabbed his work bag and Max put on his backpack. After taking a quick glance around, Morris spoke into his watch.

"Granny, Emmanuel, are we set?"

"Set and ready to roll," replied Granny.

"Mia?

"Ready to rock."

After taking several deep breaths, Morris and Max walked to the main entrance of the large, rectangular red-brick building. It was ugly in contrast to the magnificent structures around it. At the entrance, as they figured, they were stopped by a security guard.

"We're from Data Computer Systems. You called us about some computer problems?" Morris showed the head guard his company badge. The man analyzed it for several seconds, frowning at their obvious youth, but finally nodded and motioned them to follow him. *Computer work might just be the only area where youth is not a liability,* thought Morris with satisfaction.

"We have a glitch in the system. This is the first time since your company installed it. I'm getting no reception from the cameras in several areas, including the west wing. I need to have those cameras up and running as soon as possible. After testing the alarms, which I do periodically, I found that they're not all working either."

"We'll take care of it. We'll flush out your system and see what the problem is. If you can take me to the main terminal, I can start working there. My assistant will need to walk the grounds to check the cameras and the wiring to make sure nothing's wrong with them. I hope you made lots of coffee. It could be a long night."

Morris smiled. The man gave him a strange glance before turning away. Morris and Max followed quietly as they headed to the main office.

The computer room was nestled behind the main office near the center of the building. When Morris entered the room, he could see the double row of screens, which featured several areas of the grounds. The majority of the screens were showing static.

"Well, what do you think?" asked the guard.

"Don't know yet. I'll need to check the wiring to know more." Morris turned to Max. "Why don't you start with the cameras in the cemetery. That seems to be where the problem is. There are at least ten cameras or so out there." Morris then turned to the guard. "Sometimes all it takes to mess up the system is a few corrupt wires. Weather can affect them, as well as rodents. We'll check those wires thoroughly."

Morris said to Max, "Make sure you keep me posted."

Max nodded and walked towards the hallway.

"The kid can't go by himself," said the guard. "I'm the only one on duty tonight. The other guy had to leave because he was ill. I have the rest of the grounds to check before going back to the cemetery."

"So you secured that area already?" asked Morris.

"Yeah, but still, you'll have to wait before going over there until I can secure the other areas."

"I can take him," supplied a sweet voice. Liliana popped into the room from around the corner. "Someone in my last tour group forgot their camera, Luciano. I just came to retrieve it." Liliana held up a camera case to show the guard. "I have no problem showing this guy around if it'll help you out. Anyway, I owe you for taking care of that disruptive fellow in my tour group earlier today."

The guard narrowed his eyes. He seemed to be considering letting Liliana help him out, but he clearly had his orders, too.

Morris folded his hands over his chest. "If we have to wait, maybe we should just come back another time. I mean we've got other calls we could be handling, you know. Time is money. Yup, that's probably the best course. We'll just pack up and come back another day. How about next Thursday between ten and four?"

Panic lit the guard's eyes. "But we have to have those security systems on line now. We have to."

"Oh, I get that. It's just not my problem you're short handed." Morris patted him on the shoulder.

That seemed to push him into a decision. "All right! Fix the computers. Do what you have to do. Go where you have to go, but stay to the corridors. They're lit in all areas. The cameras are near the top of the walls. You know where they are, Lily. Call me if you need anything." The guard handed Liliana a radio.

Liliana took it and smiled sweetly at the guard. She then turned towards Max. "Ready then?"

Max nodded and followed her into the hallway. After a few minutes, Morris and the guard could hear Liliana talking about the building and its history. The sound of her voice was reassuring and calming. After several minutes the guard turned towards Morris. "I need to check the other buildings. I'll be back shortly."

"Hey, do whatever you need to do," he said. "I'll be here."

Morris started removing the panel where all the wires for the computers were kept. Once the guard left, he felt each wire until he came to the one he was looking for and placed a plastic clip over it. He then reached into his bag and pulled out his laptop, testing the connection. He now had access to the security system and could see the various cameras. "Granny?" Morris whispered.

135

"We're in, dear. I can control the cameras."

"Liliana did some fancy computer work to sabotage the system like she did, but I'm working on correcting the problem right now." Morris tapped on his keyboard, and easily found the problem she had built into the system. After several minutes he had it figured out. "The system's clean, and now we have eyes everywhere."

Max called in. "Can you see where the guard is?"

"Yup," said Morris. "I put a tracking device on his shoulder. He's heading for the Opera Museum of the Cathedral. You have plenty of time before he gets back."

Morris smiled and said, "Max, you and Liliana are on."

MAX SMILED. "OKAY, LILIANA, show me what we're doing here." They had walked past the chapel part of the cemetery, a fenced-in area separated from the other buildings by a line of trees, they headed toward an entryway. On each side of the cemetery were two doors, but it was open on the inside. The entryways had two-panel doors that were usually locked, but the guard had left them unlocked, so they could have access to the cemetery cameras he knew weren't working.

They pushed open the dark mahogany doors that creaked with weight. As they walked through the entryway, Max had to stop, his eyes wide and full of amazement at the sight before him. The walls of the cemetery were loaded with statues and sarcophagi. The floor was a brilliantly clean multicolored marble that echoed with every step. The corridors resonated with light, and they could see for quite a distance. In front of them was a walkway that led to the central courtyard, an area with lawns and eroded stone bases. There was a slight chill in the air as a breeze wafted over them from the courtyard through the open windows.

"It's over here." Liliana whispered as she led Max to the end of the long cloister to their left. Once there, they turned right and stopped towards the middle of the cloister, where a group of statues stood or leaned against or near the wall. Among them was a tall ethereal one. Along each cloister were some uniquely painted frescoes, and flush with some areas of the floor were tombs with effigy reliefs. "Here it is—the statue of Leonardo Pisano, better known as Fibonacci."

Liliana stood back while Max analyzed the white statue. The figure was in a traditional pose, with Fibonacci standing tall, a book in his left hand while his right hand was open and slightly extended. His face was handsome and confident. He wore a long robe draped loosely, and a hood that covered everything but his face. The statue seemed to be in pristine condition, except for missing fingers on each hand, which showed the scars incurred during World War II. Though, as Max studied it, expert restoration made it look practically undamaged.

Max raised his hands and put them on the solid white stone base that stood half his height. The statue had a base of white marble with the name "Leonardo Fibonacci." Below that, inscribed on a different type of stone, was the following:

A
Leonardo Fibonacci
Insigne Mathematico
Pisano
Del
Secolo XII

Which translated to:

A
Leonardo Fibonacci
Mathmatical Insigne
Pisa
Of
Century 12th

"Technically, that information isn't accurate," said Liliana. "Leonardo lived from about 1170 to the 1240s. His books were produced starting in 1202, during the first decades of the *thirteenth* century."

Liliana kept her voice soft. Max looked over and felt every inch of that base, finding nothing. He was disappointed, knowing he was probably missing something. He took several steps away from the statue but didn't notice the tomb in the marble floor behind him close to the wall of the cloister. His heel landed in the cavity there, causing him to fall back, throwing his weight off balance. He fell.

Liliana rushed forward. "Are you okay?"

Uninjured, except for his pride, and feeling particularly awkward, Max nodded as he jumped up. He quickly dusted himself off and turned to see what he had tripped over. The cover of the tomb was silver. The picture on the tomb was of someone lying in a coffin— reclined and with hands folded over the stomach. A book rested under the hands. The head was placed upon a pillow, while the feet were barely covered by the long robe lavished over the body. The person's features were peaceful and resolute. Surrounding the edges of the tomb were carved words in Italian along with Fibonacci numbers.

"Liliana, is Fibonacci buried *here*?"

"Not that I'm aware of. To be honest I haven't noticed this tomb before. There are so many around here that it's hard to keep track."

"If he is not buried here, then why would a tomb of him be here?"

"I guess I don't know. It makes no sense to me," answered Liliana.

"What does it say?" asked Max as Liliana moved closer to read it. She read in Italian, "'*Un uomo saggio si preoccupa non per quello che non può avere.'* It's an Italian proverb. It says, 'A wise man cares not for that which he cannot have.'"

"That sums up a lot of truth right there, doesn't it?" Max knelt down and passed his fingertips over the numbers. He noticed that all of them were boxed except that the eight and thirteen appeared cleaner than the rest

"Granny?"

"I'm here," responded Granny quickly.

"Did you come across any proverbs in the journal?"

"We found lots of interesting information. Proverbs? There's one in Italian near the last page."

"What did it say?"

"Well," began Granny. "It says, 'A wise man cares not for that which he cannot have.' Does that mean anything to you?"

Max grinned. "It sure does!"

"We also noticed a pattern. Eight and thirteen are seen throughout the journal," chimed in Emmanuel.

"Thank you so much for that bit of information, Emmanuel, and thank you too, Granny."

After several minutes of pondering what to do, Max pressed on the eight and thirteen with his fingertips, testing a theory. A loud report echoed through the cemetery, and Max and Liliana glanced around to make sure they were not heard. The disruption of the quiet was only a moment, ending with the sound of escaping gas. Realizing that the large tomb door was not going to lift by itself, Max leaned down and grabbed the edge.

The cover was heavy and cold as Max flexed his muscles and lifted. The cover gave way to stairs leading into a dark abyss. Cobwebs lavished the entry way.

"Did you know about this?" asked Max.

"No," said Liliana, "I had no idea. But tombs don't have rooms underneath them like this. Even though I wasn't aware this was here, it wouldn't surprise me if Grandfather knew about it."

"I'd say it was certain he knew. Dante knew about it because he sent us here," replied Max. "He wants us to find something."

Max took out a flashlight and shined it down into the hole. Taking a deep breath, he took his first step. Then another. Liliana tentatively followed. With each step, Max could feel a coolness wash over him. Unlike the cool breeze from outside, it chilled him to the bone. It was the coldness of death. At the bottom of the stairs, Max splashed the beam of the flashlight around a small room. He noticed two tall candles on either side of the wall ahead. Solid wax flows covered the sides of each candle, indicating they'd been used before.

Max took some matches from his backpack and lit the candles. He waited, almost expecting something to happen, but nothing did. The passage went below the base of the statue. Max glanced up and could see the Fibonacci numbers wrapped in a large circle, as if they were indicating something, like an X on a pirate map. Max reached into his backpack and pulled out a hammer.

"What are you doing?" asked Liliana.

"I'm going to smash a hole in this wall."

Liliana protested. "You can't! What if you're wrong and there's nothing behind that wall? Do you have any idea how much trouble you can get into for destroying architecture in a museum?"

The urgency in Liliana's tone caused Max pause. "Do you think this secret room would be down here if there wasn't something behind it?" After several seconds, Liliana conceded.

Silently, Max said a prayer before bringing his arm back, but before he swung it forward, something on the wall caught his attention. The Fibonacci numbers seemed to move and wiggle. Max lowered the hammer and handed it to Liliana, stepping closer to analyze the wall. It was an illusion, he was sure of it and yet even now there was nothing he could see to cause the effect. The numbers appeared to change shape. The zero in front grew larger while the numbers at the end grew smaller. A line appeared on either side of the numbers, forming a long slender skin. Now the circle appeared to be a serpent on the prowl, its mouth open ready to strike, and in the center of the circle appeared a mouse on the run.

Max ran his fingers over the numbered serpent.

"Liliana, did you see that?" After several seconds without a response, Max looked behind him. Liliana had her finger in the air, pointing at the wall. She was speechless. "Yup, you saw it," Max confirmed as he returned his attention to the wall. "Let me see. A serpent would eat the mouse, so how do we get it there?"

Max touched the number zero and pressed on it, moving it sideways. Amazingly, it moved quite easily, as if on wheels. Max carefully glided the numbered snake towards the mouse, moving it into several circles before finally accomplishing the goal. Once the mouth of the numbered snake was on top of the mouse, he heard a click. Max slid his hand down the wall. When it landed on the mouse, Max could feel it give. He pressed on the mouse firmly.

A loud grinding came from the wall, and the large circle fell inside the wall, landing on a track, which caused it to roll out of the way. Max cocked his head, leaned forward and stared at the circle's retreat.

"Max!" gasped Liliana. "Look in the hole!" Max quickly raised his head and focused his gaze on a small treasure chest set into a rectangular space inset in the wall. It was smaller than the hole, which was about two feet in diameter, and covered with dust and cobwebs. Max made the necessary checks to make sure there were no surrounding traps, then reached inside the hole and grabbed the chest by its two side handles. Max lifted gently, his muscles flexing and back straining from the effort. The chest was surprisingly heavy. Max exhaled. The fact that the chest was heavy was reassuring. If it had been very light, Max would have been concerned that it had been relieved of its contents. Heavy, he hoped, meant the items they were looking for were tucked safely inside.

Max was about to remove the chest from the hole when he heard Mia's voice through his watch phone. "Max, get out of there! Get out of there now!" The urgency in his sister's tone caused Max to forcefully yank out the chest while shouting to Liliana to grab his backpack. Liliana did as she was told, blew out the candles, and followed Max up the stairs and out of the grave opening. Max immediately began to close the heavy cover of the tomb.

"What's going on, Max?" Liliana was scared. She began to repack Max's backpack, putting away the flashlight and hammer.

"I don't know. Calm down. We'll be fine." Max talked into his watch phone. "What's the problem, Mia?"

"Did you find anything?"

"Of course, but—"

"Good, because we have company at the security building. The guard went to check it out but ended out in a heap on the ground. We saw three people through one of the cameras after they blew a hole in the side of the building. Max—it's Denton. He's here with Willard and Theryn. Don't let them find you, please."

"It's too late," murmured Liliana as she glanced through one of the windows towards the far entrance.

She could hear the creaking door before she saw the three men pouring through the entryway, looking around them frantically.

"What about Morris? Where's he?" Max continued in a whisper.

"He's already en route. He was able to get out the security room before Denton got to it. All of his equipment was with him, but he still thought it'd be fun to force Denton to find a way into the room on his own." Liliana and Max glanced at each other. "He sabotaged the door."

Max nodded and told Liliana. "He can't use force to open it because of the equipment, cameras, wiring. If he destroys it, he'll have nothing."

"I know a way for us to get out of here undetected," she said.

Max picked up the chest and his backpack. "Show me!" he said as he glanced down the long empty cloister.

Liliana led the way, trying to stay out of the intruders' sight, who were still standing in the same spot wondering which way to begin. Then they both heard the order. "Theryn, start on the right. Willard, begin on the left. I'll search the courtyard. If they're here, we'll trap them like rats."

Theryn and Willard skulked off towards their assigned areas.

In the center of the cloister was a magnificent statue reclining on a large base. It was a sarcophagus.

Max scanned about. Upon seeing no one, yet knowing the enemy was closing in, he focused his attention on the statue. Behind the figure was a two-foot space. Liliana placed her hand on the statue's marble pillows. A section slid to the right, uncovering a keypad. Liliana tapped in several numbers then replaced the section. Max glanced at Liliana in surprise.

Liliana glanced to her right, then her left, before walking closer to the wall. She tugged Max with her.

"There they are!" yelled Theryn, and Max could hear him running down the cloister towards them.

"Hurry!" urged Max as he watched Liliana push on the wall. A door opened, and Liliana ducked through it, vanishing as if by magic. Max could not believe what he was seeing. "What is this?"

"Our way to freedom," came Liliana's voice from the shadows. Max took a deep breath before glancing one more time at Theryn racing towards them. Max followed Liliana, stepping through the sheer portal with as much courage as possible. He disappeared almost instantly, leaving nothing for Denton and his accomplices to find. The stone wall became hard again. They heard a loud thud that Max hoped was Theryn hitting the wall as he tried to follow. A second thud soon followed. Very satisfying.

Max could see nothing but could hear Liliana unzip his backpack. She pulled out the flashlight and shined its beam in front of them. The walkway was narrow and long. The ceiling was low, and they had to duck as they proceeded or hit their heads on rock. This made carrying the heavy chest rather arduous. The path in front of them veered to their right and moved downward, going underneath the cemetery into a hole of darkness the flashlight seemed to have a hard time penetrating. If there was something dangerous ahead, Max feared they wouldn't see it until it was too late.

"How did you know about this?" whispered Max as he followed Liliana. The chest, held tightly to his chest, was fatiguing his arms. He could feel his muscles burning under the strain.

"There are many secret tunnels and passageways among the walls and grounds of the Camposanto Monumentale. You'd be surprised how much they're used too."

"That door appeared to be magic. What was that?"

Liliana glanced quickly at Max, a smirk on her lips. "What you saw was an illusion. You of all people should know better than to believe what you see."

SIXTEEN

"WHERE ARE THEY?" ASKED MORRIS as he glanced at his watch nervously. Twenty minutes had passed since Mia had contacted Max and Liliana. Since then they had not heard from them. Morris had been able to barricade the security office quickly once he heard Denton arrive and felt the vibrations of the exploding wall. Denton knew how to make an entrance if nothing else. Mia had given him a heads-up when the trio had moved on, allowing him enough time to escape, but now Morris worried that Liliana and Max had not been able to do the same. He feared they'd been caught and were at the mercy of Denton and his accomplices, who, when they couldn't get into the security room had proceeded to the cemetery.

Mr. Weedlesome, Morris, and Mia were waiting in the van. Mr. Weedlesome had moved the van closer to the exit near the Opera Museum, ready to dash away at a moment's notice. All eyes were focused on the courtyard and the other attractions, wary of Denton and his buddies, hoping to see Max and Liliana. Mr. Weedlesome, his grip clenched tightly on the steering wheel, waited for his moment as wheel man.

He'd had an idea of what Morris and the rest of the Crypto-Capers team usually did on an adventure, but now that he was actually part of one, he found it nerve-wracking. He gave this bunch of "kids" a lot of credit for what they did and, which was his concern at the moment, not folding under pressure. He'd have to see his therapist when he returned home. At that moment Mr. Weedlesome, glanced to his right and saw two figures exiting the base of the Tower of Pisa. "The tower!" he yelled.

Morris and Mia turned around quickly. Max and Liliana were running hard, had almost reached the van, and Max was holding something. Mia and Morris opened the right side door of the van allowing them to vault inside. With chests heaving, they collapsed in a heap on the floor, while Morris slammed the door closed behind them.

"Go, Mr. Weedlesome!" panted Max, "and fast. They're on our tail."

Max fought to catch his breath, but his heart felt like it was in his throat. Liliana panted, and sweat poured from her brow, her chest heaving from her exertions.

Mr. Weedlesome threw the van in gear and stomped on the gas. Tires squealing, the van leaped away. The passengers were slammed back against their seats. He was, perhaps, taking the role of wheel man a little too far.

Once they were on their way, Morris lifted the chest out of Max's arms so he and Liliana could get tied into their seats. Mr. Weedlesome wove through the night, his erratic driving soon calming and blending with traffic after the first panicked rush away from the cemetery.

"Ah, where should we head next?" he asked.

"Back to the hotel," said Max. "It's time for plan B. I contacted Granny and Emmanuel. They'll be ready with all our stuff outside the service entrance. We need to head for the airport and get out of here as soon as possible."

"How do you know there aren't other clues for us to find here?" asked Mia as she glanced apprehensively at the chest.

"I'm confident that this holds the answers," Max said, patting the chest. "More to the point, Emmanuel does."

Morris and Mia glanced at each other before returning their gazes to Max. "As we agreed, Morris, Liliana, and Mr. Weedlesome will remain behind, while the rest of us return to Chichen Itza and finally resolve the issue with the treasure."

"What of Dante?" asked Morris.

"Oh, he'll show himself again. I'm sure of that. But right now he's counting on us to find the Golden Monkey. At the same time, we're hoping to capture the most notorious villain that ever lived."

Max stared out the side window, watching the blur of the street lights zooming by.

"Do you think the Panther will show?" asked Mia, as she placed a hand on her brother's shoulders.

Max huffed a laugh. "I *know* he will! The man's that greedy, and . . ." Max paused. More softly he added, "And he has a score to settle."

Max glanced over his shoulder at Mia and gave her a weak smile. The case was wearing them down, that was for sure. They were exhausted, and yet determined to continue with what needed to be done. When this was over, they'd definitely need a vacation.

"Don't worry, Mia. He won't win," said Morris. "Instinct will force him to come, but, believe me, we'll have the upper hand." Morris's reassuring smile soothed Mia.

Soon they arrived at the service entrance of the hotel. Granny and Emmanuel were waiting for them, all their bags packed and piled. Morris and Max hopped out to help load everything. Within ten minutes, they were on their way again, this time to the airport.

SEVENTEEN

FOR SOME TIME, NO ONE SAID anything. There were questions each one wanted to ask and yet no one really wanted to ask them. Finally, Emmanuel couldn't contain his curiosity any longer.

"What *is* that?" he asked, indicating the chest.

Max roused himself from his thoughts. "We found it by the Fibonacci statue, in a secret room under one of the tombs. This chest was hidden down there."

Emmanuel's eyes grew large, and he raised his fingertips to his lips. "The chest of mystery!" he said, his tone hushed.

All eyes were on Emmanuel now. "What's the chest of mystery?" asked Max.

"It was a . . . was a . . . actually it was a bedtime story my grandfather told me when I was a child. It was a sought-after chest no one could open, except the one person it was meant for. Only that one person was destined to use what was inside. Grandfather would always make me the hero of the story, telling me that I would one day open the chest and use the contents to accomplish a specific, an amazing goal. I didn't believe him, of course, well, not really. I mean, I did as a little boy, but later I laughed at the prospect of being a hero of anything, except in my dreams—especially after his stories of the chest. Only in his stories *was* I the hero opening the chest and saving the world from evil."

Liliana reached out and placed her hand on Emmanuel's shoulder, squeezing gently. She said, "Grandfather told me those stories, too, except in them I was not the hero. You were. Only you. Emmanuel, you *are* the key. Look at this chest. There's no lock or key hole to open it. It *is* the chest of mystery. Grandfather, the Crypto-Capers team, and I, have been trying to keep you safe and away from harm—there's a reason why."

Liliana motioned to Morris. He placed the chest in Emmanuel's lap, then patted him on the shoulder. "Only you can open this chest, mate, and find out what's inside. No one else in this van can do it. This chest is special, just like you. Open it, Emmanuel, and complete your destiny."

Emmanuel was afraid, uncertain. He didn't know what was inside, yet he hoped it was what they needed to open the treasure room. He took several deep breaths, knowing he was the focus of everyone. Emmanuel raised his hands and brought them closer to the chest, but the closer he came to touching it, the warmer his hands felt. It was a strange feeling. All eyes were focused intently on the chest. Unbelievably, just like in Dante's stories, it was changing colors. Emmanuel withdrew his hands slightly, and the color returned to the dark brown of aged wood.

"Keep going, Emmanuel," encouraged Morris. "It's working."

Emmanuel pressed his eyes shut a long moment, then again moved his hands closer to the chest. He felt as if there were a force pushing against his hands, but eventually he could touch it. When he did, the chest changed to a steel grey, and large, intricate-looking squares formed on the front of it. On each one of these squares were letters. But the letters didn't make sense.

Mia placed her hand on Emmanuel's shoulder. "It's a word scramble. Would you like me to help?"

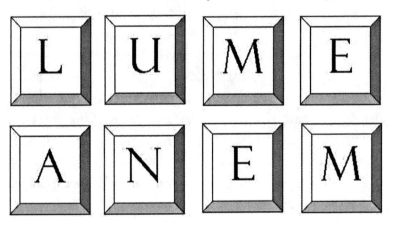

Emmanuel shook his head, and tears sprang to his eyes. "Grandfather told me the person meant to open the chest would have his name appear on the front." He glanced up at Mia. "I need to solve this one on my own."

Emmanuel began to arrange the letters. The letters weren't fastened to the chest, only set in the square frames, so Emmanuel could move them from one place to another. When he had put them into an order of his choosing, the letters vanished. In their place appeared three more squares, but these contained two numbers and a blank.

"The Fibonacci numbers," whispered Morris. "They keep showing up. Why are they used so often?"

The question was actually a brilliant one, though Morris spoke out of frustration, but Emmanuel had an answer. "Grandfather loved my grandmother and his brother very much, and though Marcello and grandfather fought constantly, it doesn't mean they didn't love each other. What happened to them was really a tragedy. It was part of a cycle that could never end. After their death, Grandfather relived the pain that greed had caused, and what it had cost him—his family." Emmanuel breathed deeply, almost not being able to continue.

"For years my father and grandfather had been locked in verbal war. My father told him it was time to move on and forget the past. It had consumed Grandfather for too long, and he could see it was destroying him. The problem with the past, though, is that you can't forget it. You have to learn from it. Because of my grandfather's sins, our families have been in hiding. We used to live in Italy when I was younger but moved to South America when people started coming after us seeking the treasure. We vowed to watch over it, see, and yet stay clear of it at the same time. Liliana's family is hiding in Spain for the same reason. Grandfather's sins have punished us all, and my father hates him for it." Again, Emmanuel took a deep breath.

"Marcello and my grandmother both died on the thirteenth day of the eighth month of the year. That's why we see those numbers constantly. They are to remind Grandfather of his sins. And yet with death comes rebirth. My birthday is on the thirteenth of March, while Liliana was born on the eighth of May."

"Oh," said Morris. That cleared up a few unanswered questions. Silence reigned for a few minutes before Morris brought up another question. "What about the blank box on the chest?"

"A thumb print?" said Emmanuel with question. "I remember Grandfather said something about the hero's thumb print being needed to open the chest."

"Of course," commented Granny. "A thumb print is a person's unique identifier. If Emmanuel wasn't the one to open the chest, it would never unlock. Your thumb print is the key."

Emmanuel swallowed, then placed his left thumb flat on the square. He pressed down on the eight and the thirteen at the same time. Instantly, everyone in the van could hear the chest unlock. The top swung up on its own.

Emmanuel, who saw what was inside first, raised his hand to cover his mouth. Inside of the chest, lying on a bed of dark velvet, lay the tablet of the eagle next to a circular object very close to the shape of the sundial, but there was a clear crystal set in its center. There were some Spanish words etched above the crystal as well.

"The sundial Grandfather gave me should sit between the tablets, Mia. From the pictures you took of the treasure room wall, it shows a similar picture, so that's where that sundial must go, while this one must be placed somewhere on top of the ruins to absorb the light from the sun and, somehow, send that light to the sundial down inside."

"I knew there had to be something else used in this sundial equation," said Mia, beaming.

Just then, Mr. Weedlesome screeched to a halt on the tarmac beside the plane that had brought them to Italy only the day before. It was ready to take off.

"Have a safe trip back to the Riviera Maya," Mr. Weedlesome said. "Morris will be checking on your progress frequently once he arrives home, while I . . . well, I'll be at my therapist. This was way too much excitement for me."

The levity brought some smiles, quickly followed by hasty good-byes. Granny hurried them along. "We have to go, and quickly. We have no time to lose. We don't know how close Denton is."

Morris reached to shake Max's hand, slipping something into his palm. Max glanced at it in question.

"You'll get it in time. Be ready," said Morris softly.

Max wasn't sure what Morris was talking about, but he trusted him. Without question, he put the note into his pocket.

The Crypto-Capers team quickly loaded onto the plane, making sure they didn't forget anything. Emmanuel kissed Liliana on the cheek, whispering his thanks. He then closed the chest and, carrying it, followed the team onto the plane. Within ten minutes, they were up in the air and on their way.

EIGHTEEN

THE PLANE LANDED ON A LONG, narrow strip of grass
in the jungle close to Chichen Itza. They didn't want to
risk the notice of landing at an airport. Memories of
what happened a week ago filled everyone's mind. They
had left on the run, the Panther on their heels. Now he
was likely hiding in the Riviera Maya, awaiting their
arrival, with spies posted at every turn. Morris had contacted the team before their landing, warning them of
this. Back at the Holmes' residence ahead of their arrival
in the Yucatan, Morris had all his equipment up and running, and the Panther's tracking device shined brightly on
his computer screen. He would follow the action from
that safe base. He also had a message for Granny, direct-
ing her to a metal shop not far from their hotel.

The Crypto-Capers team and Emmanuel took
only what they would need from the plane. Granny, Max,
and Mia stocked their backpacks with the tablets, the
sundial, the bejeweled circular piece found in the chest,
along with other equipment they thought might come in
handy. The hotel they had stayed in was on the other side
of the archeological park, and Emmanuel needed to go

back there. Granny volunteered to go with him. She said she needed to retrieve something, something Morris had waiting for them.

It was risky to split up, and everyone knew it, but there was little point dwelling on the matter. As Granny and Emmanuel set off down one path through the trees, Max and Mia headed straight for the Carocal.

The air was thick with heat and humidity, and already their clothes were becoming drenched with sweat. They had to plunge through trees and tangled under-growth to make it to the ruins unseen. It seemed to take them a long time, but soon they made it to open ground where the ruins could be seen clearly.

"This way," said Mia, after they had scanned the area for trouble. "The main temple is to the left. If I remember correctly, the Carocal is ahead of it."

The pair proceeded in that direction, but just to make sure, they contacted Morris to verify their position. "Can you see us?" asked Mia, waving her right hand to the sky.

"Stop that," said Morris. "You'll attract attention. Of course, I can see you. You're going in the correct direction. It's just ahead. I see a few tourists but nothing like the throngs we had last time. By the time you make it to the Carocal, the people inside should have moved on." Morris paused for a moment, clearing his throat. "I must say that I do prefer being in the background. Safer that way, you know." Suddenly, Morris sneezed loudly.

"Bless you, mate" offered Max.

"Thanks! My allergies kicked up. Darn it, and I was doing so well, too." Max and Mia glanced at each other and laughed, shaking their heads. It was just like old times.

"Thanks, Morris. How are Granny and Emmanuel doing?"

"Making progress! They're almost to the hotel. They'll be on the grounds in, five . . . four . . . three . . . two . . . one. They're near the stable now, towards the back of the property. They made good time. The plane landed closer than I thought. When I found that landing strip, I knew it was close, but it was hard to tell just how tough the terrain would be. I'm good!"

Mia rolled her eyes as they continued toward the Carocal. They saw a few tourists near the ruins, taking pictures of the structures with their families mugging for the cameras in front of them. At the Carocal, as Morris had predicted, there were no tourists around. Before they entered the portal, Max bumped against Mia with his arm. "Ready for a little climbing, are we?"

Mia knew exactly what Max wanted to do. The crystal sundial would have to be placed somewhere towards the top of the ruin. The problem was, they weren't sure where. Mia took some belaying lines from her backpack and tied one end into a loop. She then brought it up, and after a few twirls, lassoed the highest point of rock above the shadowy entrance, catching it onto a thick edge of rock. She attached a climbing harness. Mia was the lightest, so she started the assent up the side of the Carocal. Mia was swift and made it up smoothly. Once on top, she began to scan for a place where a sundial would go.

"Anything?" called Max.

Mia started to shake her head, but then raised her hand and carefully moved towards a thin piece of rock towards the center. There was a circular hole near the top that could be seen from both sides of the rock.

"I think I found it!" she said, excited. "There's this piece of rock that . . ." There was no way Max was going to be able to see it, so she aimed her watch towards the rock and quickly snapped a picture of it. "Look at your watch!" Max glanced down and saw the picture.

"Perfect! Now what?"

"Well," Mia began. "These ruins were built towards the rising and the setting of the sun. So the only way this sundial should be able to work is when the sun first hits it in the morning or at dusk, and sundown is fast approaching. Contact Granny and let her know that she and Emmanuel's time is running out."

Max immediately contacted Granny through their watch phones and told her the news.

"I'm on my way back now. Emmanuel's father wanted him out of harm's way. There was no point arguing. They've gone into the tunnels behind the store where they'll be safe. I got what we needed!"

"Good! About Emmanuel, we shouldn't need his help any longer, anyway. The rest we should be able to figure out on our own, don't you think?"

"We'll know soon enough. I'll be there momentarily. I'm getting a horse."

Max looked back up at Mia. "Be careful when placing the sundial."

"I will," replied Mia as she removed the crystal sundial from her backpack. She placed it into the hole, turning it slightly to the right to make sure of its fit. Mia was sure she had found the right place when she heard the sundial lock into place. She then stepped back and turned to face the sun. The sundial was definitely in the correct position.

"Are we set?" called Max.

"Yes!" Mia answered.

"Good. Now come down from there. We'll head inside and see if we can't get a head start opening the treasure room."

Mia carefully lowered herself down. Once her feet landed, she instantly unhitched the rope and followed Max into the shadowing doorway that led inside the Carocal. A fading light filled the walkway. When they reached the first room, memories of the meter-long iguana made her look around in case it had returned.

"You can go first," offered Mia sweetly.

Max glared at his sister, knowing full well why she didn't want to go into the room.

"I have an idea," said Max as he removed a flashlight from his backpack. He turned it on and shined it all around the room several times until he was assured there were no hidden beasties lurking about. Pleased,

Mia hurried inside and walked straight to the impressions on the wall.

"Max, the tablets, if you please."

Max removed his backpack and opened it. He gently lifted out the tablet of the jaguar, carefully placing it in Mia's outstretched hands. The tablet definitely had some weight to it, and Mia flexed her muscles to lift it to the impression on the wall where the jaguar stood. The tablet fit perfectly. She heaved a sigh. In a whisper, she said, "Now the next one!"

Max took out the tablet of the eagle and carefully handed it over. Mia raised the tablet to its place in the impression on the wall where the eagle flew. It also fit. Mia then went into her backpack and took out Emmanuel's sundial, placing it in between the tablets. Instantly, Max and Mia heard something lock into place.

"Emmanuel was right," Mia commented.

"So far so good," said Max, staring at the wall.

"Now, according to Dante, when he and Marcello opened the treasure room the first time, there was nothing inside." Mia pulled out Marcello's journal and began to look at the marked pages where Emmanuel had placed sticky notes. "So far we've done everything they did. We placed the tablets where they belonged, then put the center sundial in a position to connect everything together. The sundial is in the correct place up top, too. As far as I can tell, we duplicated what Dante and Marcello did to open the false treasure room."

"Agreed! Now what?" asked Max.

"I don't know. When the light hits that crystal sundial on top, it'll open the false treasure room, and I don't know how to change that to open the real treasure room. There's nothing else here that tells us to do anything differently."

Max stepped closer to the tablets and noticed that, though they were locked into place, there were not molded into one piece. Max analyzed every crevice and placed his hand on the sundial.

"If I were a Mayan, I would've created something different. An extra step, if you will." Max pressed on Emmanuel's sundial with his palm and heard something else click. At that moment, a bright light came from the top of the wall, blazing its way down towards the tablets. It looked like molten lava.

"Max!" said Mia as she pointed towards the ceiling with her right hand, her left hand grasping Max's wrist. They watched what was happening with amazement. When the light flowed into the tablets, they appeared to glow a fiery red. The tablets seemed to come to life and attack each other on the stone. The eagle flew and attacked the jaguar with its sharp talons. The jaguar seemed to be at its mercy but then summoned all its strength and hit the eagle with his gigantic paw. When the eagle was down, the jaguar roared loudly. When that happened, the ground shook.

Mia and Max stepped back. At first they thought it was an earthquake, and almost bolted out the door, but then they realized that just the ground moved and not the walls. The shaking was because the floor was moving.

They watched with anticipation as a narrow pillar of rock broke through the floor, rising up with the intensity of lava from a volcano. The sides of the pillar were angled and sharp. By the time the pillar stopped, it was about four feet in height. On top was a thin, narrow indention that ran deep. Max and Mia waited several minutes before stepping forward to analyze the pillar.

"That was amazing!" said Mia as she gently touched the sides of the pillar.

"I sure didn't expect that!" replied Max. "The sun setting must have caused this event to happen and yet the sun is not completely in the right position. I'm at a loss at what to do now."

"I know," panted Granny as she arrived in the entryway. She gasped, catching her breath. "Look at the cryptogram . . . from the bookmark-shaped item . . . I found at the . . . library."

Mia whipped out her notepad and found the cryptogram in question.

The page was different from when Mia had worked the cryptogram. There was a note written on the page now. It was Granny's handwriting. "I see what you mean, Granny. That key should open the treasure room."

Granny took off her backpack, reached inside and removed the black box. She hastily moved towards the pillar and looked down at the top.

"I believe I'm correct. From what Emmanuel and I read in Marcello's journal, the door should only open with the setting of the sun. Once the light hits that crystal, we only have a brief time to place the key in this pillar and open the door. Too soon and we'll just open the false room, too late and the same will happen. This pillar appeared because we are almost to that time. We must be patient and wait."

"But wait for what, Granny? Should one of us go and watch for the sunset, or . . . ?"

"I believe something miraculous will happen to tell us when that time arrives. We need to be patient and be ready to move quickly."

Max and Mia glanced at each other, their bodies tense, while Granny seemed quite calm now that she had caught her breath. She had an ability to react calmly under pressure. Granny pulled out her cell phone and glanced at the time. "Morris, how are we?" she asked.

"Almost there. Are you ready?"

Granny glanced at Max and Mia, who nodded reassuringly. "We are!" she said and opened the black box. She removed the key and studied it quickly again, noticing the dots on either side of the key handle. On the right side, there were two dots and on the left side—three. The pillar slot had the same dots carved into the stone. Granny positioned the key above the slot in the corresponding position, and took several deep breaths. Then she waited for Morris to begin the count. There was a brief pause before they heard Morris's voice fill the room.

"Ten . . . nine . . . eight . . . seven . . . six . . . five . . . four . . . three . . . two . . . one—now! The sun is in position!"

Before their eyes they saw the sundial between the tablets begin to light up. It started low, then slowly became brighter and brighter until it was almost blinding. No one could see anything.

"Now, Granny!" shouted Max. "The key!"

Granny lowered her hand, and the key slipped into the slot. She quickly turned it to the right twice and heard a click. She then turned the key to the left three times, and heard another click. Granny removed her hand from the key and waited, hoping she'd turned the key correctly. A rumble started, softly at first, but growing in volume and vibration. Stone ground against stone. Then all three saw a door appear. A door on the side of the tablet of the jaguar opened up, while leaving the tablet of the eagle closed.

"I believe we opened the correct door, team," said Max as he stepped closer. "Granny, if you will do the honors."

Granny took up her heavy pack and reached out for Max's flashlight. He handed it to her. She approached the door, then quickly vanished inside. Max followed, but Granny had stopped not far inside. From somewhere above, a light came into the room, maybe from a crack in the ceiling. The beam was not bright, but it was enough to hit a curved bowl near a corner of the room and reflect to the other corners. The beam bouncing off the bowls caused the room to fill with light, as if several light bulbs had turned on all at once. Granny was laughing.

"What is it?" Max asked.

"I'm truly impressed," she said. "The Mayans had no electricity, of course, and yet they found a way to light up even the darkest of places."

But as impressive as that light was, what it illuminated was even more amazing. The floor of the treasure room was filled with antiquities—small gold statues, glimmering gemstones, jade. Pottery of many sizes were filled with treasure, some fallen apart over time, but many still intact. There were also spears, weapons, shields, masks, and headdresses. And then there were scrolls, hundreds of them. Before them, in this hidden space, was untold Mayan history. The monetary value of such a treasure could not begin to be estimated. But what the team saw before them was not riches, but Mayan heritage, and to them the worth of that was far greater.

Mia's hand instantly rose to cover her mouth. The amount of Mayan treasure inside was so impressive that tears began to roll down her cheeks.

"We did it, Max. We did it!" she began to shout. Then Mia took a loud intake of breath. The trio continued to walk through the door and into the treasure room where they found the most impressive treasure yet. Sitting on a dais in the middle of the room was the Golden Monkey. It was a solid piece of gold molded in the shape of a monkey. Not large, it was still an impressive piece of gold. Its legs were folded, knees raised and pressed into its body while its arms were folded on its chest, its hands pressed there. It looked so real and yet it only stood a few inches tall. They all remembered the image of the monkey statue in the Van Gogh like painting in the locked library room. This monkey actually was smaller, though more detailed, and the arms and legs were positioned differently. Granny knew then that Dante, who had immitated Van Gogh's paint strokes, had never seen the real statue but was relying on legend to complete his painting. No one beyond the Mayans who had put it in the treasure room had ever seen the Golden Monkey.

Granny made eye contact with Max and Mia and quickly stepped over far greater treasures to reach this one artifact, the one thing the Panther sought above all else. As Granny made her way, she unzipped her heavy pack. While the team cared more for the rest of the treasure, they would not touch it. They would notify Mayan authorities, who would take charge of it, but the Golden Monkey . . . now that was a different story. They had gotten to it before the Panther had, but now the trick would be for them to keep it from him. That might just be the harder trick, the one part of their task that required the efforts of all of them.

Granny reached for the statue.

Max and Mia were about to proceed further into the room, but they stopped when they heard a slow, mocking clapping behind them.

NINETEEN

"WELL, WELL, MY DEAR MIA and Maxwell. I do hope you enjoyed the theater tickets I left for you in Las Vegas. I must say, those Devereaux sisters can really entertain. I was going to ask you before this, but I wanted to mention it to you . . . in person."

Mia whirled and stared at the Panther in amazement. He didn't look like the man they had met in Las Vegas. Back then he had appeared almost bird like, his nose short and pointy, wearing his Tommy Bahama shirts everywhere he went. However, now he wore a partial black mask in the shape of a panther's face. Its nose was rounded and full, but with no whiskers. His eyes seemed to become one with the mask, appearing dark and round. The only part of his face that could be seen clearly was the lower part of his cheeks and lips, and they appeared sullen and hollow. His body was almost as thin as before, but no longer looked quite so frail. The Panther wore black pants and shirt, which hid much. His face was as pale as ever, though, and his back was slightly slumped. Max felt a smidgen of satisfaction, thinking that the Panther might have lost sleep over the quest.

"Yes, we did enjoy the theater. Thanks for those tickets," Mia said with some nonchalance.

"You tried to kill us," spouted Max, his eyes burning. "I thought you were more civil than that."

The Panther scoffed. "Don't be silly. If I'd really tried to kill you, you'd be dead, dear boy. The explosion on the plane was only a distraction, at most a kind of test to see if you were really worthy to face me. Did you think that I didn't know you'd probably be able to find a way out? You have eyes in the back of your head, remember?"

Max knew he was referring to Morris. The Panther stepped forward carefully. For once he seemed to have no accomplices with him, which was odd. He usually prefered minions to do his bidding. That he faced them alone probably meant he felt absolute certainty about the outcome of their encounter. Max knew they still had an ace up their sleeve, but its effectiveness depended on timing. Always it was about timing. He stepped forward to meet him, wanting to focus the Panther's attention on him and nothing else.

"You see, Max," said the masked man, "I have this . . . dependence on your team. It sickens me really. I'm the most notorious villain who ever lived. I'm always one step ahead of all authorities around the world, and yet I find myself at the mercy of you . . . mere children!"

The Panther turned his head away in disgust, but before he did, Max could see the admiration he felt for them in his dark eyes. It was almost too easy for Max to rub salt in the wound. "The irony of our situation is that our very youth gives us the strength and courage to be able to defeat you."

The Panther's head snapped back to Max, his eyes narrowed behind the mask. Then, without warning, he snaked out a hand and wrapped bony fingers around Max's throat. With the intensity of the panther he was portraying, he rushed forward, slamming Max's body against the nearby stone wall. Pain etched Max's face at the impact.

"Don't underestimate me, foolish boy. I'm not above crushing you like a bug beneath my feet. I'm not beyond killing you, so don't mistake my weakness as feelings I might have for you. I'll admit I wish you were my own children, instead of my own bumbling son. I admire your brilliance and determination. You could be such a criminal, so unstoppable if you had a smidgen of ruthlessness. Instead you insist on being an agent of good. Such a waste."

"Think what you could do if you—"

"No! Never! I can't be changed. I don't want to! I've lost all hint of compassion years ago. If you think of me as anything not cold and hard as stone, you'll lose. I won't lose sleep over your deaths now."

The Panther began to squeeze Max's throat, cutting off his air. Max tore at the hand at his throat. Mia rushed forward and grabbed the Panther's arm. "But you'll miss him, Julian. If you kill Max, you'll miss him." Her soft tone caused the Panther to loosen his hold.

"I don't go by Julian Cross anymore, Mia."

"I know it wasn't your given name," she added softly, "but inside, inside I believe you *are* Julian in so many ways. His talents embodied you."

The Panther took a deep breath and glanced at Mia, his features remaining firm. He then brought up his other hand and caressed her cheek. "If I had a daughter, you would be she." He then paused for several seconds, dropping his hand. "But I'm not that man, so don't play mind games with me."

He then turned his attention back to Max and his grip tightened on Max's throat again. But then, rather than pressing his advantage, he lifted him and threw him to the ground. Max landed with a *thud*, and he gasped for air. Mia turned to go to him, but the Panther stopped her. "You'd trade your life for his?"

Mia gazed in amazement at the man in front of her. His audacity was unnerving. "Would you honestly take that trade?"

The Panther gave a cryptic laugh. "Not today, my sweet, but eventually you'll leave me no choice."

"Then you're not the man I thought you were. You're no man at all. You're a monster!" Mia raised her hand to cover her mouth.

He laughed. "Good, I'm finally getting it through your head. I'm not your friend, Mia. Not someone to be manipulated and used."

"And we are?"

An evil smile played across the Panthers lips. "Oh, my girl, you fail to see the most obvious of things."

The Panther loomed closer to Mia, forcing her backwards until her back hit the stone wall behind her. But that wall was as far from the treasure room door as Mia could manage.

"The day your team loses its usefulness," the Panther continued, "is the day you die. You only stay alive because I need you to be. It's twisted, I know, but it's true. At first I wanted to destroy your team, but you proved your usefulness time and time again. Over and over I've used you to do what I could not. Now I'd sooner destroy a priceless painting than you. So we're connected, if you will, and if I go down, so will you—and hard. But, keep in mind that I've destroyed priceless art before. So you can keep coming after me if you want, and in truth, I know you will, and that's the joy of it all, isn't it? But the repercussions go beyond us."

Mia narrowed her eyes.

"So," the Panther said with an evil grin, "what have mummy and daddy been up to lately?"

The full meaning of his threat penetrated her very soul like icy fingers. "You wouldn't go that far. This has nothing to do with our parents." Tears began to fill Mia's eyes. As one lonesome fat tear rolled down her soft cheek, the Panther caught it with his fingertip.

"What makes you think I wouldn't include them? My son was an innocent causality."

"He's a criminal!" spouted Mia. "I wouldn't say he's innocent. He committed crimes to please you. He deserved to be in jail, but you fixed that didn't you?"

"He's still involved."

Mia breathed deeply, forcing her fears to flow from her like steam.

"We won't give up our hunt for you. You'll go down and go down hard. I'll see to it personally that you'll rot in jail for the rest of your days. How dare you threaten me and my family."

The Panther laughed eerily, causing fear to rise again in Mia's chest. "Pursue this course, and the first one to suffer will be your . . . grandfather." He said this with sinister humor.

Mia's eyes grew wide. "My grandfather? Are you nuts! He's dead. Good luck with that one."

Arrogance filled the Panther. He leaned toward her, rubbing his cheek against hers and whispering in her ear. "Do you honestly believe that he's been dead for the past five years? It's rumored that he drowned in Venice, right?"

Mia began to shake her head. "You lie! You don't know what you're talking about. That information could have been found anywhere." Then she heard something that caused her to grow cold.

"Harold slipped and hit his head," the Panther said. "He fell into the water that day. Oh, yes. That's true. He would have drowned, too, if I hadn't saved him. I was there, you see. I was the reason *he* was there. He was chasing me, of course, but, as always, I was one step ahead of him. When I revived him, he had no memory of his previous life. I convinced him that he worked for me, and, as a criminal, he was . . . miraculous. I could never have gotten this far without him. You see . . ."

Mia was no longer listening. She did not want to believe what he was saying. Her grandfather was working for the Panther? He wasn't dead? The news was too much to handle. She tried to cover her ears to the Panther's gloating, but he grabbed her wrist. As he pulled at her arm, he brought his other pointer finger up and tapped Mia's nose with it.

"You need to hear the truth," he said with a grin. "When he got his memory back, Grandaddy confronted me. Ha ha. That's when I used a threat to you and your brother to persuade him to continue as before. So you see, killing you now would be pointless. I need you alive!"

Her face filled with anger, Mia brought her hand back and swung, smacking the Panther across the cheek. The look of conceit was wiped clean from his sallow face and the mask went crooked. Suddenly that narrow jaw tightened, and the Panther knocked Mia to the ground. But Mia had been trying to provide the exact right distraction. Max was sneaking up behind him. But just as Max was ready to lunge, the Panther kicked him hard in the chest, sending him sprawling onto the ground.

"Are you quite finished?" demanded Granny from the treasure room doorway. In her hands, she held the Golden Monkey. The gold glowed in her arms. It was impressive this statue, larger away from the other treasure.

"Hello, Nellie. A pleasure, as always," said the Panther making a mock bow of gentlemanly respect.

"You must know that your time is almost up. Morris has notified the authorities, and if my calculations are correct . . . and they usually are, they'll be here in less than five minutes to put your sorry self in prison." She then held up the statue. "You came here for this, didn't you? Take it. Leave and take your chances with the police."

"Do you want me to believe that you're just going to hand it over to me? After all we have been through, Nellie? I don't think so."

"This means nothing to me, but those children do. Take the blasted thing and leave them alone. This is your one and only free pass. The next time we meet, you'll go down, even if I have to take you on myself."

He grinned. "I'd love to see that show, dear woman, you and I battling each other."

"Keep up harassing my grandchildren, and you'll see it sooner than you expect. I guarantee it'll be a bigger hit than your show in Las Vegas."

Granny's features were stone, her anger filling every crevice and wrinkle. By herself, Granny figured the Panther would believe he could take her, but something inside of him prevented him from trying. He snatched the Golden Monkey from her. It was quite heavy, but he held it tight and bolted from the room. Granny dashed to Mia first, then, once being assured that she was okay, went to Max.

Granny heard sirens in the distance, but she was sure the Panther would get away. In fact, she was counting on it.

TWENTY

DAYS PASSED BEFORE DANTE DE LUCA came out of hiding. The mishap at the cemetery had been plastered all over the news the day after the Crypto-Capers left, with investigators looking into the details of it. Dante knew they would find nothing of consequence. The rest of the week had been quiet. It had taken him several days to reorganize his house and fix the damage the thugs had done. Liliana had even come over to help with the many repairs. When it was complete, Dante was eager to get back to his own peaceful life.

As he looked around, his thoughts flew—as they had often—to Morris and what he and his team were up to. During the week he had seen nothing on the television about the treasure, which made him believe that the Crypto-Capers team hadn't been able to find it. Breathing deeply with disappointment, he sat down in front of the picture of the Chechen tree and stared at it, his left hand at his forehead. It was then that he heard a knock on his door. He quickly rose from his chair to answer it. He was hesitant to open the door, remembering vividly the encounters with the Panther and, later, his thugs.

After taking several deep breaths, he placed his hand upon the knob and turned it.

When he opened the door, he could not believe what he was seeing. Emmanuel was standing there, with the chest of mystery in his hands, and standing next to him was his father, Dante's own estranged son. Tears ran down Dante's cheeks. He had not seen his son in years. Emmanuel had brought them together. Dante reached out and fiercely wrapped the two in a bear hug.

"My son! Emmanuel! I'm so glad you're both here." When Dante released them, he clasped their cheeks in his hands before letting them go.

"Dad," said Emmanuel's father as he smiled and walked into the house. Emmanuel waited.

"You put a lot of trust in me, Grandfather," said Emmanuel softly. "It means so much to me."

Dante patted Emmanuel on the head and smiled.

"You earned that trust, Emmanuel. I hope you now understand why I did what I've done. The secrets and the lies, and about my brother and your grandmother. I have an ugly history. I hope you and your father can forgive me." Dante grew quiet.

Emmanuel offered him the chest of mystery. "This is for you, Grandfather." Dante lifted the cover off of the chest and gazed at its contents. Inside were all of his and Marcello's belongings that the Crypto-Capers had borrowed or found to solve the mystery. There was also a piece of paper. Dante lifted the paper and read it quietly. It said:

Dear Dante,

I first want to thank you for everything. You have helped us solve the Legend of the Golden Monkey. Directly and indirectly of course, but know that the job is done. The Panther is on the run, but will not be bothering you anymore. We found the treasure! This I know will interest you. The Golden Monkey is real and the treasure room also contained amazing artifacts that were still intact. The Mayans owe you a huge piece of their history. Your belief in the treasure made this all possible. Though we discovered the treasure, you and Marcello are the ones who will get the credit. I told you we were not in this for the treasure or for the glory. We are treasure protectors. Here is the percentage the government gave us for finding the treasure, minus our expenses of course, and thanks for the generous bonus. I hope the satisfaction of what you've done warms your heart and heals all wounds. Your family is your greatest treasure. Take care of them. Farewell, my friend, and if you need our services again, please don't hesitate to find me. You know how.

Sincerely,
Morris

Dante glanced past the letter and found a pile of pictures. His eyes focused on the top one. It was of the Golden Monkey, a statue quite different from his imaginings, but wonderful nonetheless. Underneath that was a bank note receipt, a deposit in a Swiss bank. The amount was staggering, many millions. Tears sprung to Dante's eyes. Emotions he could not explain, choked him. After several minutes he raised his face to the sky and cried, "It's over, Marcello! It's finally over!"

TWENTY-ONE

SOMEWHERE ON THE OTHER SIDE of the world, the
Panther sat in the sun on a tropical beach staring at the
Golden Monkey and praising his own good fortune, listening to the soothing sound of the ocean curling against
the sand, when he felt that something wasn't right. In an
hour he was to meet his buyer, a greedy man who loved
artifacts of any kind and who had jumped at the chance
to purchase the famed Golden Monkey. What he'd do
with the artifact, the Panther didn't care. After he handed it over, he only wanted to relax in a style the wealth
from the sale would afford him. His feet propped up on
a chair as he stared at the peaceful blue sky.

For weeks he had kept the Golden Monkey hidden, afraid the Crypto-Capers would suddenly appear to
relieve him of his prize. But they hadn't. Sure that he had
made good his escape, he basked in the afternoon sun
and caressed the artifact, fantasizing about what he
would do with his money. That was when he felt something on the back of the monkey's skull. The Panther
immediately turned the statue and looked. On the back
was indeed something, a button. Without thinking twice,

he pressed it. As soon as he did, the Golden Monkey broke in half with a hiss of escaping air. Two things immediately became apparent. One, the Golden Monkey was not solid gold, was in fact mostly made of lead, and, two, it had a piece of paper hidden inside. Anxiety rising, edging toward panic, the Panther grabbed the paper. It was a *typed* letter. It said:

Dear Panther,

In the end we knew you'd hold out for the Golden Monkey. It was only a matter of time. Your persistence is admirable. As you must know by now, however, what you possess is not the real Golden Monkey. Granny made the switch while Max and Mia distracted you. None of us knew what the real one looked like, but, hey, the fake is much larger, more enticing for you to possess. The real one is safe from you now, in a high security secret location where you can't get it, and, when you try—and we know you will—you'll be caught. The South American government expects you. Oh, and the buyer you're dealing with knows the truth, too, so you may as well forget your meeting. He's already flown the coop.

At that moment the Panther received a text on his phone, confirming the cancellation of the meeting. He was furious, but he finished reading:

You'll find that your avenues of escape are dwindling. It would be in your own best interest to disappear for a while, probably a very long time. We've beaten you again, and though we know you'll release your revenge upon us when the time is right, we'll be ready. As far as you're concerned, we won't give up trying to stop you. When we meet again—if we meet again—you'll be caught, either by us or the police.

On a more pleasant note, here are two tickets to the Opera House. We hope you enjoy them just as much as we enjoyed the ones you gave to us in Las Vegas. We know how much you love the theater, so we wanted to return the favor. You should have no problem getting there in time.

As always our best wishes,

The Crypto-Capers

The Panther was amazed, not quite sure how he was supposed to react. He looked underneath the letter and saw the two tickets to the Sydney, Australia, Opera House. From where he sat, it was less than an hour to the theater.

"How did they . . ." But then a smile spread on his lips. His eyes filled with delight, as if he knew a secret. Then, without warning, he began to laugh, a cruel and body-shivering laugh that promised redemption.

THE END

Check out the next adventure in the Crypto-Capers series. EHT EASC FO HET KOAPCCE SIADERI!